MISTS OF
GARIBALDI

Tales of the Supernatural

MISTS OF GARIBALDI

SHERRY BRISCOE

MISTS OF GARIBALDI

Tales of the Supernatural

SHERRY BRISCOE

Chat Noir Press
P.O. Box 663
Eagle, ID 83616

http://ChatNoirPress.wordpress.com

For Ann Rutledge - this one's for you Mom.

MISTS OF GARIBALDI

SHERRY BRISCOE

Table of Contents

MISTS OF GARIBALDI

MOONSHADOWS

Reason will dictate that the only way to escape from misery is to recognize it, and go the other way.

Even the wind, which always blew, was stagnant that day on the courthouse steps. Zoey Jacobs shoved through the crowd as Anthony Todd Pierce, convicted serial killer, made his way into the brutal August sun. With his hands cuffed behind his back and microphones shoved in his face, he showed no remorse for the twelve lives he'd stolen. He smirked at Zoey, his bushy black eyebrows raised, insinuating he knew something she didn't. Her stomach churned.

Zoey snapped pictures of the man of contrasts, his paper white skin and swarthy black hair. She turned away in disgust. Her steps were halted as the convicted killer whistled a tune from her childhood, *Row, row, row your boat gently down the stream, merrily, merrily, merrily, merrily, life is but a dream.* Each note vibrated through her nerves and settled in her bones.

Bang! Screams and gasps erupted from the crowd as Anthony Todd Pierce collapsed on the steps. Blood seeped across the front of his orange jumpsuit, his eyes fixed on the open sky. Zoey swung around, not missing a beat, and snapped the front page shots of the murderer-turned-victim, the spectators, and the chaos, while police swept through the crowd hunting the shooter.

Zoey snapped another shot of Pierce lying on the cement steps. She stuffed her camera in its bag, slid her press badge in a pocket, and backed away. In the eight years she had worked for the *Times-News*, she had never witnessed anything like this.

The whistling echoed in her ears as she drove to work.

Zoey sat in the crowded editorial room to type the story, but her shaky hands wouldn't cooperate. Her mind was clouded with streaks of blood dripping down the courthouse steps. The newsroom was filled with ringing phones and chattering people. She needed to get away from the confusion and the noise. She grabbed her gear and quietly exited out the back door.

The viewing platform at Shoshone Falls provided stability. Zoey inhaled the splendor of nature as a rainbow hovered above the pulsing waters. Shards of colored light dangled, suspended in a bank of mist. Her shoulders relaxed and chest expanded in a more peaceful rhythm. The roar of the rushing water washed away the pandemonium of the morning.

Photography was Zoey's refuge, a source of sanity against the windy desert of south central Idaho. She studied the water as it tumbled over the edge of the falls. Her mind sorted through photo options. She could catch each drop in perfect clarity, or move the shutter speed just enough to make it a soft blur of motion. Her thoughts surrendered themselves to the dance of light. She adjusted the shutter speed, shot, and did it again.

Squinting her eyes against the bright sun, Zoey slowly scanned the horizon for any shape, color, or lines she might have missed. Life was a picture through the lens of her Nikon D90.

Carefully putting the camera in its bag and condensing the tripod to fit neatly back in its case, Zoey packed up her gear. She slipped off the fly-fishing vest her father gave her as a birthday present several years earlier. It came in handy on shoots with pockets for lens caps, pens, and filters. Zoey jotted down notes indicating dates, times, locations, light, shutter speed, aperture and lenses used. She shoved the note pad and pen back in their pocket, picked up her camera equipment and headed up the pathway to her Subaru.

Wouldn't it be nice, Zoey thought as she carefully stepped across the rocks, if she could fix her life the way she fixed her pictures? If she could crop cancer or heart break, the way she could crop an empty can from a pristine landscape, she would have her mom back, and stop worrying about her dad. But life was not a photograph, and destiny was not contrived through software.

Zoey found herself contemplating why she stayed in this desert hamlet she called home, while aspiring to a life on distant shores with salty air and endless waves.

It was nearly six o'clock. Zoey's father would be standing in the kitchen, no doubt, drumming his arthritic fingers on the counter. He was taking her out to dinner tonight. It was August third, and Zoey was thirty today.

Holding the screen door so it wouldn't slam as she entered the old house, Zoey peeked around the corner into the kitchen. Her father wasn't home. She put her purse on the counter and ran upstairs to her room.

Zoey looked at her suitcases resting in the corner of the room, picked up the boarding pass from the desk, and smiled. This time tomorrow she would be in Portland, Oregon. The ring of her cell phone jolted her back to the present. She rushed downstairs and answered out of breath, "Hello."

"Zoey, this is Doctor Bundy. I just wanted to let you know your father is in the hospital. He's had a mild episode, so I'm keeping him for a couple of days."

She crumpled the plane ticket still in her hand and let it drop to the floor. Zoey's heart fell with it. "I'm on my way." She brushed her tears aside as she ran to the car.

The large and uninviting entrance to the Magic Valley Hospital loomed on the canyon rim. Zoey rushed through halls and into the room where her father lay.

A nurse in green scrubs stood beside him looking at the monitor and taking notes. "Press this button if you need immediate assistance, otherwise I'll be back to check on you soon."

Zoey nodded at the lady as they passed in the doorway. She smiled at her father. He was the only family she had, and while she could leave him, she could not lose him. She walked over and sat in the chair beside his bed, and looked at him sternly. "What happened? And don't leave out a single detail."

Stan Jacobs placed his old weather-beaten hand over hers, his arm colored with a calico tattoo of age spots. He smiled gently. "Zoey, I'm okay, baby girl. An episode, nothing more. Doc just wants to keep me for observation."

Zoey frowned. "You mean you had another heart attack? This is the third one, Dad."

Stan's gentle old eyes met with hers; he smiled. "Just an episode. You have a plane to catch in the morning. I've got Joe next door to keep an eye on me while you're gone."

Zoey swallowed the bitter choice she'd made. "No, I'll wait. There's always another time."

Her father coughed. "We are not having this argument. You're going."

"You're right, Dad. We're not having this argument, because I'm staying. But I am a little miffed that you're not taking me out to dinner now for my birthday!" She forced a smile.

He closed his eyes and shook his head. "I'll take you out after you get back from Oregon."

"We'll see what the morning brings. Right now you need to rest." She sat back and looked up at the wall-mounted television. "Anything good on TV tonight?"

That night, Zoey lay in bed looking at glow-in-the-dark stars that had been on the ceiling of her room since she was a little girl. Memories of family laughter, her mother's perfume, and Sunday dinners danced through her mind. Moving back in with her father was meant to be temporary while he recovered from his stroke last winter. Now she wasn't ready to let go, yet it was all she could think about. She drifted off to sleep.

Zoey saw herself standing on the canyon's rim, surveying the edge of the world through her camera lens. Across a river of darkness sat a house that rose out of a mist. It was an old white farmhouse with blue and green trim. A golden retriever sat on the edge of the porch that spanned the front of the house. A light in an upstairs window flickered and then went out. A strange looking wind chime danced in the breeze. She turned her lens to bring the house into focus. She snapped a picture - crack! Tiny lines exploded like a spider's web. She gasped at the shattered lens!

Zoey bolted upright in her bed. She wiped her wavy red hair out of her face and looked around the room. She heaved a trembling breath, "It was only a dream."

The full moon filtered through the lace curtains that gently rippled in the night air. The clock next to her bed showed three a.m. Zoey made her way to her desk, turned on her computer, and opened the folder of pictures. If she couldn't sleep, at least she could get some work done. One by one she adjusted balance, saturation, mid tones, highlights, and clarity. Here she was in total control.

Zoey admired the image of the Perrine Bridge majestically spanning the Snake River. But something was out of place. She clicked to enlarge the picture once, then again. Part of a metal object blocked the view of the bridge's lower left bracing. She searched her notes, no mention of anything unusual.

Next she reviewed a stunning aerial shot of Blue Lakes Country Club golf course in the canyon. She enlarged the picture again and again. There was another piece of metal obscuring the image, similar to the first, but different.

Clicking through all the shots, Zoey noticed every one revealed a small section of a metal object somewhere in the frame. Her frustration mounted. She clicked the program's selection tool and outlined each errant piece putting it in a new window, matching lines, curves, and reflections of light to piece the puzzle together. After adding the last section, she sat back and beheld the striking metal sculpture that leapt in an explosion of waves on her screen.

Zoey was getting a headache from trying to figure out what was going on. Perhaps she should be the one in the hospital for losing her mind she thought, as the machine clicked off and the room filled with silence.

Zoey crawled back into bed and turned her head to the open window where a hummed melody drifted on the night air. *"Row, row, row your boat."*

The blood in Zoey's veins froze. She separated the curtains and scanned the yard and road beyond, but couldn't see anyone in the dark. She shut the window and locked it.

The morning sun flooded Zoey's room. She sat on the edge of her bed eyeing the suitcases taunting her from the corner. "Why is it so hard to leave this place?" she asked. She hated the desert, was drained by the inability to escape the gossip and drama of the small community surrounded by sugar beet factories and dairies. She wrinkled her nose. The smell of neither pleased her. Dressed for the day, she tossed her robe over the suitcases, slipped downstairs, grabbed her car keys, and headed out the door.

Zoey walked into the hospital room as they were serving breakfast. She smiled at her dad. "You have a little more color in your cheeks today; they must be treating you right."

"They won't let me have any bacon, and they left half the egg in the kitchen. A person could starve in a place like this."

"A person could get healthy on food like that." Zoey laughed as she moved the newspaper plastered with her photos from the courthouse steps the day before, and sat in the chair beside his bed.

"Aren't you supposed to be on a flight about now?"

"No, I'm supposed to be right here with you. Besides, I have some pictures that messed up and need to be retaken."

"The pictures in the paper look fine to me."

Zoey glanced at the newspaper. "Not those, some other shots I took."

"You take pictures all the time. You must have a million by now."

"Nope, only nine hundred thousand. I still have a few more to go. What's the doctor say?"

"Oh you know, he thinks I'm a pretty good lookin' guy for my age."

"I mean about your heart."

"Oh that. They got some tests and all that stuff. Probably go home tomorrow."

"We'll see." She winked at him and kissed his cheek.

In the afternoon as her father rested, Zoey retraced her steps from the day before, taking the same shots, from the same angles of the same locations. She made sure nothing unusual showed in the lens. The second shoot was normal with only what she intended.

On the third day Zoey brought her father home from the hospital. She planned a nice quiet lunch for the two of them. She set up TV trays, one in front of her dad's recliner and the other in front of the couch beside him. She covered them with nice linen place mats and napkins, ice tea, and lunch. She held her glass up. "Here's to another year together, Dad. I love you."

Stan groaned a little as he sat up to do the same, then eased back into his chair to eat his salad. He looked over at Zoey and smiled. "Baby girl, I know how much you want to leave this place. Why don't you just get in your car and go? Drive to Seattle, or maybe San Francisco. See the world. You don't have to stay here."

"Dad," she shook her head. "Maybe my need to stay is greater than my desire to go?" She set her fork down. "Don't worry, one of these days the right opportunity will come along, and then you'll be missing me."

Stan smiled in his understanding way. "Zoey Nichole, I will always miss you, no matter what. But like your momma always said, you gotta' let go and see where the wind takes you." He coughed and cleared his throat. "Now tell me about these messed up pictures you were talkin' about. Did you get them fixed? Is something wrong with your camera?" He took a bite of chicken.

"My camera's fine. It was a fluke really. The other day I had some double exposures." Zoey explained the pieces of the sculpture and how they showed up in different frames.

Stan smiled, "Reminds me of what your mother called a moonshadow."

Zoey's forehead crumpled up with question. "A what?"

He put his fork down, "I think it was a story from her childhood. The moonshadow was like a shared image between two people."

"What kind of image?" Zoey questioned.

"If I remember right, it was like if I was out in the field looking at a tractor, but thinking of her, then she would see the tractor, or whatever I was looking at."

"She would see it where?" Zoey asked.

"She would see it as a reflection in glass, water, any smooth surface. And she said it was the moonshadow, a shared image between two soul mates."

"Did you two ever have that happen?"

Stan smiled. "One time when we were newlyweds, she said she saw it. I don't even remember what it was. But the important question is, what did you see?"

Zoey held on to her glass with both hands as if it was an anchor. "I saw a metal sculpture, a beautiful piece that looked like a half moon, a star and an ocean wave bursting through it."

Her father smiled. "And who is your sculptor?"

She shook her head. "I don't know any sculptors. There's nothing like that here."

He prodded further. "Then where?"

Zoey's heart skipped a beat. "I don't know. But it doesn't matter anyway. He's not here and I'm not there, wherever there is!"

"You have to get over this notion of yours that you can't leave this valley."

Zoey stiffened up. "You know what happens when I try to leave. People get sick, have strokes, die." Her words were so final; to her they were carved in stone. Her mother's headstone.

"Dear, I had a stroke the first time you bought a plane ticket, but I came out of it. Your mother died the second time you bought a plane ticket. She had cancer. That's what happens. The world will not end if you buy another plane ticket."

"Where would I go?"

He scowled. "Go and find your sculptor. He needs you."

Zoey sighed in exasperation. "You need me. Besides, I wouldn't know where to look."

He leaned forward in his chair and wiped his mouth. "Then stop looking, and let him find you."

After Zoey helped her father to bed, she sat in her room scrolling through images on her computer screen searching for the ghost that haunted her lens. She opened the file with the sculpture and traced the lines of it with her finger over the monitor. She could almost feel the sharp cold edges of metal, its curves and the way it weaved around.

Nine o'clock Monday morning Zoey walked in the back door of the newspaper office, and set her camera bag down on the edge of her desk. She sifted through a stack of papers in her basket and skimmed through endless emails.

Sandy Miller, her editor, leaned against the edge of Zoey's desk.

"They're still looking for the shooter from last week." She said.

Zoey twitched a little, startled. "Huh?"

"You seem a million miles away. What's on your mind?"

Zoey rubbed her tired eyes. "The ocean, salty air, strange sculptures." She laughed.

Sandy handed her a rolled up magazine, leaned over and whispered in her ear, "Remember what we talked about last week? Check out the classifieds." She smiled and walked back to her office.

Zoey flipped through the pages of the magazine, scanning the ads. Her eyes stopped on a notice for a photojournalist circled with a yellow highlighter.

The Headlight-Herald in Tillamook, Oregon needs an experienced photojournalist to join their small team.

Zoey stuffed the magazine in her camera bag and sprinted out to her car. She nearly hyperventilated at the thought of leaving Idaho. What if her father had another heart attack? Her thoughts bounced back and forth between hope and anxiety. But fate didn't yield to fear. She picked up her cell phone, barely able to hit the numbers with her nervous fingers.

"Hello. I'm calling in response to your ad for a photojournalist." Zoey listened with anticipation as the woman on the other end described the position in the small coastal town. It sounded perfect. "Yes, I can email you a resume and work samples this evening. Thank you." She ended the call and dropped the phone on the seat next to her.

Wednesday evening Zoey set the dinner table. She and her father sat down to pork chops, mashed potatoes, and corn on the cob.

"Life is good," Stan said as he filled his plate.

Zoey's voice was a bit shaky, but she had to get the words out before she changed her mind. "Dad, I've got a job interview in Oregon."

Amazing, she thought, as she watched the sadness in his eyes even while he smiled. "When?" he asked.

"Friday. I'm driving."

Thursday morning just before dawn, Zoey packed her car up for the trip - her iPod, some trail mix, her cell phone, and of course a map. She hugged her dad good-bye and half expected something to stop her from leaving, car problems maybe, or the house exploding, but nothing happened. The wind blew the sagebrush across the open desert as Zoey drove to her future, the coast, and a destiny that had called to her in a dream. She drove to the ocean.

The sun was just setting when Zoey pulled into Tillamook, Oregon. The newspaper office was closed. The streets were quiet. A seagull screeched not far in the distance. She stood on the sidewalk, closed her eyes and smiled as she filled her lungs with the coastal air. She was in love. Could her soul mate be a place rather than a person? She wrapped her arms around herself and walked along the sidewalks, peeking in storefront windows.

Zoey's heart stopped as she peered in the window of a small gallery. The metal sculpture stood beneath a single spotlight in the center of the room. She could almost hear it whisper on the cusp of the wind that touched her wavy hair. She tried the door, but it was locked. She had to get inside; she had to find out who made this work of art, this creation of metal that held her soul. She strained her eyes at the placard by the piece. The sculptor's name was too small to read. But the title of the sculpture took her breath away. In large bold letters it read, MOONSHADOWS. She felt her entire body tremble; her knees could barely hold her up.

A couple walked past and smiled. "Lovely pieces, aren't they?" The woman commented.

Zoey couldn't take her eyes off of it. "Do you know who the sculptor is?"

The woman stopped and looked in. "I'm not sure, but isn't that one of Leon's pieces?"

The man thought for a moment, "Leon Price?"

Hope filled Zoey's eyes. "Does he live around here?"

"Garibaldi," the woman said, "just around the bay." The couple nodded and walked on.

The next day Zoey whistled a joyful tune as she strolled down the street to the *Headlight-Herald* office, housed in a century-old building that was in need of new paint.

Gail Conway, the publisher, sat at a large old wooden desk in a small alcove of the office. The high ceilings were framed by ornate trim. Gail sipped her coffee and sorted through several piles of paper in no specific order. She stood to greet Zoey, handed her the current issue of the newspaper, and sat back down. "You understand Miss Jacobs, we are a weekly publication. The *Headlight-Herald* has a long history in this community. It was first printed in the late 1800's."

Zoey nodded in understanding. So it wasn't the *L.A. Times*, she thought, but it was the Oregon coast. She giggled inside.

"I do have one more interview and will be making a decision by the first of next week. But so far, I will say, I am very impressed with your work." Gail smiled and pushed the dull frizzy hair out of her face. "Are you staying a few days, or heading right back?"

Zoey looked at the paper and back at Gail, "I had planned on spending the weekend here, seeing the sights. Any suggestions?"

Gail handed her a copy of the *Oregon Coast Magazine*. "This issue comes out once a year, has all the information you need. What there is and where it is." She rubbed her chin and the one hair that poked out from it. "You picked the right time of year to visit."

Zoey sat in the parking lot skimming through the *Headlight Herald.* His name, it was his name, right there – in the obituaries. Leon Price, died of natural causes in his art studio on Tuesday, August third, at the age of 73. Zoey's heart sank lower than she thought possible. She read on. "Leon is survived by his daughter Maria of Vancouver, Washington, and his step-son, Carter Webb of Garibaldi. A reception for friends and family will be held Friday."

Zoey dropped the paper. That's today, she thought, I have to go to his reception.

She started her car and drove along the Oregon coast highway around the bay to the little fishing village of Garibaldi. A haunting mist hung over the water. Zoey felt for a moment as if she were driving through a different dimension. She turned right on First Street following the trail of bright yellow balloons tied to small posts in the ground, as the road curved around the far edge of town. A two-story house sat on the right, with a large barn on the left. Several cars were parked in between and people walked around the grounds, and in and out of the barn.

Zoey sat in her Subaru for a moment, mesmerized by the house. It was an old white farmhouse with blue and green trim, and a wraparound porch. She grabbed her camera and ventured into the barn. A golden retriever greeted her inside. She smiled down at him, "You've been waiting for me, haven't you?" She petted the friendly dog.

Inside, people wandered around, looking at the most striking pieces of sculpture she had ever seen. Old pieces of wood and metal had been given new life by this old man's hands. She walked through the crowd as if she had known them for years, as if this was her home.

A man stood behind her and held out a bottle of beer. "Want a beer?" He wasn't much taller than her, but stalky with wavy blond hair that rested on his shoulders.

Zoey twirled around. He was so close she could smell him, inhale his wonderful aftershave mixed with the sweat in his clothes. It made her smile. She took the bottle of beer without a word.

"My name's Carter. I don't think I've seen you around here before?" Each syllable he spoke was a beat of her heart. His eyes sparkled.

"My name is Zoey Jacobs. You knew the sculptor?" Her eyes followed the lines of his face, his dishwater blond hair, and the gentle lips that smiled at her.

Carter took a drink of beer. "I'm his son. Most of these are my pieces; Leon taught me everything." He tapped his left leg which gave a metal sound. "Even made my own prosthesis."

Zoey looked at the ankle and noticed it was metal. "Oh, I'm sorry."

Carter laughed. "Nothing to be sorry for. Just part of life." They smiled, drank and watched the art of life weave around them through the mingling crowd.

"Do you mind if I ask you about a piece I saw in Tillamook? A sculpture called Moonshadows."

Carter's eyes softened with sweet memories. "That was Leon's last piece. I took it over to the gallery August third, the day he died."

"What did you think of when you looked at that piece?" Zoey's heart began to race.

"Leon always said that piece was about destiny. I guess it was that. Leon always saw the art of a piece, and I saw the science of it. That piece I'd say for me was about connection, the way everything came together in it. Destiny, purpose of life, I don't know. But it is a special piece for sure."

But in the midst of life stands death, and there he was too. Zoey dropped her bottle when she saw Anthony Todd Pierce walk through the middle of the crowd and flash his crooked smile at her. His left eyebrow furrowed up, he whistled, "*Merrily, merrily, merrily, merrily, life is but a dream*".

Zoey trembled, unable to catch her breath. Carter put his hands on her arms and pulled her to face him. "Are you okay? What's wrong?"

Zoey's heart resumed beating, her lungs resumed breathing. She looked back in the room, but he was gone. She had watched that man die, she was sure of it. Her eyes drifted back to Carter. "I'm so sorry, I thought I saw someone. But it must have been my imagination. I'm sorry about the bottle." She reached down to pick it up. Carter knelt down with her.

"Don't worry. There's plenty more. I hope you'll stick around?"

"Yes." Zoey said, as she stood back up, and cautiously peeked around the room to see who might be looking back at her.

Is there ever an end?

THE KILLING SUITE

Look forward, walk in confidence, with happy hearts that beat in hope and do not pound in fear.

Zoey stood at the front desk of the Garibaldi House Inn and Suites, which by the way was the only hotel in Garibaldi. It was late and she was tired. "What do you mean you have no rooms? I have a reservation."

The middle-aged woman behind the counter poked a pencil in and out of her beehive hairdo. "I'm sorry Miss, but your room wasn't guaranteed with a credit card. So when you didn't show, we gave it to someone who did."

"Do you have any rooms?" Zoey squeaked through a yawn as she shifted her weight from left to right.

"No, like I said, we're full."
Zoey rubbed her tired, droopy eyes. "Is there any…"

"None!" The clerk snapped, impatiently tapping the pencil on the counter.

Zoey narrowed her eyes at the clerk. "Where can I get a room tonight?"

The desk clerk shrugged.

"What about rentals?"

The desk clerk laughed. "This time of year? On the Oregon coast?"

Zoey's voice tensed. "Any bed and breakfasts around?"

The desk clerk winced and rolled her eyes. "The Garibaldi B&B. Though it's not really a place I'd want to stay."

Zoey grabbed the handle of her small suitcase. "You think they have a room?"

The desk clerk nodded. "As long as you don't mind sleeping with ghosts."

Zoey headed out the door. "I don't believe in ghosts."

The desk clerk shook her head. "You will."

Heavy rain clouds hid every star from sight as Zoey drove up the road. The Garibaldi B&B was an old Victorian home perched on the hillside of the Oregon Coast highway on the southeast side of town. One light on the large porch beckoned. The parking lot was empty. She hesitated a moment as she pulled her suitcase to the porch. The weather-beaten wooden B&B sign creaked as the wind pushed it back and forth.

A cold wind brushed Zoey's face and ran its fingers through her frizzy red curls. She stopped, her heart pounding. "Is someone there?" She spoke softly, hoping no one would answer. The wind pushed a tree branch against the wooden sign. She let out a relieved breath and continued up the stairs.

As Zoey reached for the knob, the door evaded her grasp, opening on its own. She started in, but the door retracted its invitation and slammed shut in her face. Old houses, she rationalized, have such odd quirks. She looked around for a doorbell.

The knob turned again and the door slowly opened. Zoey curiously squinted her eyes to peer through the opening.

A small elderly woman peeked out at Zoey and smiled. "How may I help you?"

Zoey clenched the handle of her suitcase. "This is the Garibaldi Bed and Breakfast, not the Bates Motel, right?"

The old woman giggled as she pulled open the door and invited Zoey in. The brass bell overhead chimed when Zoey walked under it. "No Bates here, my name is Naomi."

The walls of the small lobby were covered with faded pastel floral wallpaper and age-spotted like the old woman. Zoey thought of issues of *Good Housekeeping* from the early fifties. The dust made her sneeze.

Naomi was a woman of no particular beauty, resembling an aged china doll. She wiped her hands on her apron that covered a calico dress, and took her place behind the counter.

Zoey brushed her frazzled red hair back out of her freckled face. "I need a room. I just got hired on at the *Headlight Herald*, and I haven't found a place yet."

"You want to stay here?" Naomi said in a surprisingly pleased voice. "For how long?"

Zoey looked around unsure. "Well, I need a place while I look for a more permanent place to rent. Hopefully not long."

Faint whispers came from behind the heavy drapes - or was it in the other room? Sounds moved through walls. "What was that?" Zoey asked.

Naomi gave her a questioning look. "What was what?"

"I thought I heard someone."

"There's no one else here, no one you need bother with." Naomi's head shook slightly as if she had Parkinson's. She turned around and took a key from the peg board on the wall. "If you're going to stay here a while, you'll need a larger room. I have the K suite on the top floor. But I dare say it may take you some time to find something to rent in this town." She looked over the top of her glasses at Zoey.

"Well this is where I want to live."

Naomi pushed a guest book towards her, the pages empty. "You'll need to sign in. What's your name, dear?"

"Zoey Jacobs."

Naomi looked up noticing cobwebs she had missed in the corner, then turned and headed for the staircase. "Follow me. Mind you, no elevators in this house. You don't got a problem with walking up stairs do you? And you must be quiet here. This is a respectable place."

Zoey followed the older woman up the stairs. Vintage framed black and white photographs lined the walls up the staircase. "I'm quiet, you don't have to worry about that. I love your photographs. I'm a photographer too, well, photojournalist actually."

Winged-backed chairs and a bookshelf filled a small sitting area at the top of the stairs. A double-doored entrance read "K Suite". Naomi unlocked the right door and ushered Zoey in.

Naomi flipped on the light switch. Lights flickered several times before remaining on a steady dimness, leaving dark corners untouched. Zoey set her suitcase on a bench at the foot of the bed. "It looks like something right out of the forties or fifties. I love it. It's charming." Zoey's words fell off in an echo through the large suite.

Naomi walked around the room pointing things out. "King bed, it's got its own bathroom, small but cozy. The bar was designed for entertaining with a small icebox here."

The room had hard wood floors partially covered by a faded wool area rug, and was accented by a worn chaise lounge in the corner, with a brass floor lamp standing behind it.

Zoey pointed to the curved window seat in the corner of the room. "I love that window seat."

Naomi turned to the window, her lips curled into a tender smile. "I used to sit in that window seat for days at a time when I was a little girl, reading book after book." She picked up the pastel pink and green pillows from the window seat and fluffed them, coughing a little from the dust. "Could use a fresh cleaning. I can bring the vacuum up and give it a good once-over if you'd like?"

Zoey sat down on the side of the bed, the mattress sank a bit, giving away its age. "No, that's fine. I just want to get some sleep."

Naomi shooed her off the bed and pulled the covers back. "There, you get a good night's rest and I'll clean up in the morning." She started to leave the room, and turned to look back before she opened the door. "I lock the front door at ten o'clock at night. If you come in later than that, you'll need a key to the front door as well. Will you come in later than that?"

"Yes, there may be times when I will need to come in late. But I promise to be quiet."

"Well you'll have to be quiet. I wouldn't want to disrupt any of the other guests." Naomi floated out of the room, disappearing into the shadows.

Zoey peeked through the open door, looking down the hall and over the staircase. The hall was empty and the air stale. "Other guests?" She quickly shut the door and locked it behind her. She changed into her sweats and a tee shirt, and dove into the inviting bed. The mattress sank beneath her weight, caressing her body.

Deep in the middle of the night when the full moon offered a soft glow to the room, a noise woke Zoey up. She tried to sleep through it, but a whining noise from the hall persisted. The sound seeped through the walls. Something scratched on the door. Zoey sat up. A dog at the door? The whining and scratching stopped, followed by tiny footsteps that scurried down the hall.

She rubbed her neck. "I need a drink of water."

Slipping out of bed, Zoey's bare feet touched down on the cold rug. But it was more than cold, it was wet. She walked across the room scrunching her feet from the thick substance that oozed between her toes. Flipping the bathroom light on, she reached for a towel. A pipe must have burst, she thought.

Zoey wiped her feet dry. She dropped the towel on the floor and gasped as she looked across the room and the molasses-thick blood that pooled and seeped back between the floorboards and into the carpet fibers. It disappeared as quickly as it came. She rubbed her sleepy eyes. She walked back to the center of the rug. It was dry. It must have been a dream, she thought. She forgot about the drink and crawled back in bed, leaving the bathroom light on, just in case.

The morning sun filtered through sheer drapes and drenched the room in a golden warm light. Zoey sat up and looked around. She threw the blankets back to inspect her feet and the sheets. There was no trace of blood. She shook her head at her own foolishness as she readied herself for the day. "Paranoia and the power of suggestion, that's all it was." And yet, she studied the hardwood floor and the wool rug.

Zoey heard some thumping noises in the hall and opened her door. Naomi stood smiling with the vacuum cleaner in her hands.

"Glad to see you're up, dear. Hope you slept well?" She plugged the vacuum cleaner in.

Zoey rubbed her neck. "I had the weirdest dream." She grabbed her clothes and went into the bathroom. She could hear Naomi through the door as she got dressed. Odd, she thought, that Naomi would not wait for her to leave before she cleaned. But then again, she was glad for the company.

"What you really need is a good meal. I'm cookin' a roast tonight. We eat at seven. I don't leave food out though. You eat when it's served or you eat on your own."

Zoey came out of the bathroom with a toothbrush in her mouth. "Dinner at seven. That would be great. By the way, where's your dog?"

Naomi frowned for a moment. "I don't have a dog. There's an old tom cat that frequents the back porch from time to time, but no dogs. We don't allow dogs here."

"I thought I heard … I'm sure it was nothing."

Naomi looked past Zoey to the large window seat and the leaded glass window that encompassed it. Colors and shadows moved quickly in the glass, accompanied by barely audible gasps.

Clothes on, face washed, and hair brushed, Zoey headed for the door.

"Don't forget, seven sharp." Naomi said.

Zoey walked to the corner of 2nd and Garibaldi Avenue. Smells of fish and saltwater filled the air. She stood on the corner for a moment, eyes closed, big smile as she took the deepest breath possible, expanding her lungs as far as they would go. A block down on the corner of Garibaldi and 3rd was the Parkside Coffee House. Zoey headed in for a morning latte.

A young man with multi-colored braces on his teeth worked behind the counter. His name tag read AIDEN. "What can I get you?"

Zoey looked over the menu that hung on the wall. "Good morning, Aiden. How about a Mexican mocha. That sounds great."

"What size did you want?"

"Grande."

Aiden got right to work. "One Grande Mexican mocha coming right up."

A business woman dressed in grey from her shoes to her suit, walked up to the counter.

Aiden smiled. "Usual, Miss Richardson?"

Miss Richardson had a low but stern voice. "Yes, please."

Zoey dug in her purse for exact change, and glanced up at Aiden. "Say, you don't know of any place for rent around here, do you?"

Aiden handed Zoey her cup. "Like for a seasonal rental?"

"No, I mean full time, permanent. I just moved here and I need a home. I don't see a lot of apartment buildings here, but I'd like to find something in Garibaldi."

Miss Richarson chuckled. "Apartment buildings in Garibaldi? The town council would never go for that! Where are you staying now?"

Zoey cleared her throat. "Um, Garibaldi Bed & Breakfast."

Aiden's eyes grew wide. "You actually stay there? I didn't think anyone even lived there."

Zoey choked on her drink. "No, there's an old lady that runs it. Naomi. She's okay. A little eccentric, but okay."

"Eccentric? More like batshit crazy to live in that old house." He wiped the counter down and put the money in the till.

Miss Richardson placed a five dollar bill on the counter. "I can't remember the last time I saw her actually leave the house.

Zoey nodded. "Well, sometimes people like that can be misunderstood."

Miss Richardson took the coffee cup from Aiden. "I'm sure you're right. I haven't ever met her myself, I've only heard rumors." She nodded at Aiden and left.

Zoey followed her out the door and walked back up the street to the bed and breakfast. The morning walk was invigorating. She got in her car and drove the ten miles around the bay to the newspaper office.

The *Headlight Herald* was nestled in an old building in the center of town. Zoey walked in and waved at Gail, the publisher. "Hey, how's it going?"

Gail chatted with a woman in her mid-fifties who sat across from her. She looked up a bit surprised. "I thought you weren't starting until next week?"

"Oh yes. But I came early to find a place to live."

Gail nodded to the woman who sat at her desk. "Mayme, this is Zoey, our new photographer."

Mayme shook her hand. "I write a column, *Life in the Slow Lane*."

Zoey looked at the two women. "Wouldn't know of any rentals would you?"

Gail shook her head. "Not off the top of my head. Where are you staying now? And don't tell me you're sleeping in your car."

"No, no." Zoey laughed. "I got a room at the Garibaldi B&B."

Gail looked puzzled.

Mayme looked confused as well. "People actually stay there? Live people?"

"What's the deal with that place? It's a Victorian house with creaks and groans in the woodwork, but what house that old wouldn't have noises? It's not ghosts, it's just noise."

Gail handed her a copy of the newspaper. "You mean like bump-in-the-night kind of noises? Here, find something to rent. Say, you aren't staying in the Killing suite, are you?"

Zoey wrinkled her freckled nose. "The what? I'm staying in K...what's the killing suite?" Apprehension swelled.

"Rumor has it the old lady's grandfather who built that house, had a brother in Chicago, a hit man for the Mob. And not just any hitman, but Fiore Buccieri, worked for Sam Giancana."

Zoey shrugged with a blank stare. She had never heard of Sam.

Gail added, "Albert Anastasia? One of the most ruthless mobsters during the twenties, you ever hear of him? Sam was in his family, so to speak."

Zoey smiled and shrugged her shoulders. "I get it, there's bad blood in the walls or whatever. It's a house, Gail."

Gail shook her head. "You don't understand, Zoey. Fiore, as the story goes, would come out here to visit his brother, bringing certain business associates with him. They would enter that lovely suite on the top floor, but only Fiore would come back out. None of the other people who went in the killing suite ever came out again. None!"

Gail sat back satisfied, as if Zoey should understand completely now and move her bags downstairs while there was still time.

Zoey thumbed through the paper in her hand. "Thanks, I do appreciate the concern. But I went in, and look; here I am standing on the street the next day. Rumors are only rumors, and they have no power except what the believer gives them. Maybe Naomi is batshit crazy, but she's harmless."

Mayme cleared her throat. "So you say she's just a lonely old lady in a creepy Victorian house?"

Zoey nodded.

Gail shook her head. "Well, if you don't show up for work Monday morning, I'll know why."

Zoey smiled as she looked back over her shoulder heading to the door. "Thanks for the paper. I'll see you Monday." She tried to disregard their superstitions as she stepped out into the warm sunshine. Driving back around the bay to Garibaldi, she considered what to explore next in the strange community she had come to be a part of.

Seven o'clock found Zoey sitting at a large dining room table ready for roast and wine. Her stomach grumbled. Noami had the table set as if for royalty; fine china, linen napkins, and her best silver. She poured a dark Cabernet in crystal glasses, wiped her hands on her apron, and sat down to join Zoey. She held her glass up, twirled it gently and then sipped it with elegance. Zoey smiled and did the same.

"Are the others going to join us?" Zoey asked.

"What others?"

"Other guests."

Naomi ignored her at first, cutting a bite of her roast off and savoring it on the end of her tongue for a moment before her gentle swallow. "There are no other guests. Not tonight."

Naomi took another sip of wine to cleanse her palate, eyes closed, expanding her chest.

Soft murmurs and rustling sounds from the next room startled Zoey. She almost dropped her glass of wine as she fumbled to set it down. "Who was that?" She looked back and forth.

Naomi looked at Zoey with a fierce look that scared her. "The old ones were here before I was born. They are a part of this house, like me and they can never leave. Stay away from the windows, don't get too close. Keep your distance, and they'll keep theirs. Let's not speak of them anymore."

Zoey finished her dinner in silence, not sure what was more frightening, the disembodied sounds or the woman who sat across from her. Suddenly her food had lost its flavor. She gulped.

Naomi poured more wine in both their glasses. "You're not eating, dear. You must eat. You need your strength. Drink some more wine; it will settle your nerves."

Zoey took a sip as she looked around the room again. It seemed like an eternity before she could get her dinner finished and her wine glass emptied. She got up, placed her napkin aside, and thanked Naomi for a wonderful dinner, then excused herself for the night. She reminded herself as she walked up the stairs, old houses have lots of noises, even old women can have PMS days, and there's no such thing as ghosts.

Zoey was determined to get a good night's sleep as she scrunched deep under the covers. She put a glass of water on her night stand before she got into bed, so she wouldn't have to walk across the floor in the middle of the night. Even if it was only a dream, it gave her the creeps to think about it.

A wind outside whistled around the corners of the house. Rain hit the windows hard waking Zoey from her slumber. At first she thought someone was knocking, and then she focused her eyes on the window and realized it was the rain. She rolled over and caught a glimpse of movement in the room. She gasped so fast she choked, and sat up clutching the blankets to her chin, coughing to clear her throat.

A woman in a red sequined dress with bright red lipstick to match sat on a bar stool. Three men in pin-striped suits stood behind the woman. They all stared at Zoey with an intense gaze.

Zoey sputtered out her words, "Who…who…what…?"

Their movements were spasmodic, their eyes piercing, their voices echoed.

"Free us or join us." The woman said.

One of the men tried to speak, but blood ran down his shirt from a slit across his throat, and no sound escaped from his moving lips.

The man behind the woman, slowly shook his head back and forth. "Look below. Your step reveals."

The wind picked up outside and blew a branch against the window. The loud noise startled Zoey. She only looked away for a moment, but when she returned her gaze to the people, they were gone.

Zoey tried to calm the quickening heartbeat in her chest. She slid back down in the bed, pulling the sheets completely over her head. Either she'd drunk too much wine with dinner, or she was more susceptible to the power of suggestion than she realized. Certainly the unthinkable wasn't true, there were ghosts? It was only a dream, like the bloody rug, it wasn't real, she assured herself, over and over.

In the morning Zoey pulled the sheets down just far enough to peek out and look around the room. She was alone. A shaky sigh of relief. She noticed as she looked around how the morning light reflected the old portraits hanging on the walls. She specifically noticed the large photo of a woman in a shimmering evening gown and the men in their pin-striped suits. Of course! She saw the pictures and then simply integrated them into her dream, with a little help from the Cabernet. She was sure that's all it was. She hoped that's all it was.

Zoey showered and readied herself for another day of home hunting. While she was in the room, she continually looked at the bar area to make sure there was no one else there but her.

Strolling through the beautiful back yard of the B & B, with newspaper and coffee in hand, Zoey was amazed at how inviting and peaceful it was. Stone pathways meandered through lilac bushes, rose bushes and a kaleidoscope of colorful flowers.

She followed one path to a weather-faded bench, with a stone figure of a small child-like angel sitting on the ground beside it. Zoey looked at the cherub and smiled. "Mind if I join you?" She sat down, sipped her coffee and sifted through the newspaper ads in hopes of finding a vacancy.

The fat yellow tom cat that frequented the back porch rubbed against her leg. Zoey scratched his head, he purred. "You're welcome, Tom cat." The cat jumped up and lay down beside her, soaking up the warm morning sun.

Naomi was right; there wasn't much for rent in Garibaldi. But Zoey was determined to make this town her home. She enjoyed reading everything in the small newspaper. She was lost in the weather report for the coast and the *Tillamook County Creamery Associate Names Their New CFO* article, when a strange sound startled her.

A passerby sang as he walked along the sidewalk. He looked over the fence and the flowers at her, smiled, and continued singing as he strolled away. The words to the song haunted her, "*Row, row, row your boat, gently down the stream…*" He sang softly as he turned the corner and went out of sight. Zoey dropped the paper and the coffee cup, unable to even blink. She made her way as quickly as possible to the back door of the house.

As she entered the sun room, Zoey stopped. A cold chill held her in place. She stood motionless as her eyes surveyed the room. In the far corner was an oversized mirror that reflected the light filtering in through the many windows. A strange and unnatural movement danced across the windows.

The invisible barrier holding her in place released its grip. She took in a large breath without moving an inch. Shapes darted from window to window, seeming to move only within the glass. Then, as if from nowhere, Naomi stood in the corner, in front of the mirror.

"Naomi, is that you?" Zoey croaked.

Naomi turned quickly in surprise and cleared her throat moving toward her young guest. "Just cleaning, my dear. It's a never-ending job in a house like this."

Zoey returned a nervous smile, and with a shaky wave of her hand she agreed. "Yes, I can imagine. It's such a large place, but so beautiful." Zoey looked at layers of dust that rested so peacefully, and cobwebs that hung from the ceiling. "I was just mesmerized for a moment with the way the sunlight moves through the old glass in these windows."

Naomi's eyebrows furrowed up in skepticism.

Zoey pointed to an old black and white portrait of two men that hung on the wall. "Who are they?"

"This is my grandfather and his brother. My grandfather is the one who built this house. It was his pride and joy."

"What are their names?"

Naomi looked at the photograph with a deep longing. "My grandfather was Frank Buccieri, and his brother was Fiore."

"Italian names?"

Naomi smiled. "Yes, my mother's family was Italian, and then she married Leonard Rutledge, a local man from up Washington way. He was a logger, and they lived here in the home she was born in. I was born here too."

"That's a lot of babies born in this house. Do you have any children?" Zoey asked.

Naomi's look drifted away for a moment, as if remembering something, but then it was lost. "No, I never married. This is my home, my cradle and my casket." With a most unusual smile, she looked straight at Zoey. "Will you be dining in again tonight?"

Zoey's intuition was screaming at her to run, don't stop at 'go', don't collect $200 dollars, simply run. "I'm meeting someone. Sorry, perhaps tomorrow."

Zoey excused herself and hurried up the stairs to her room. Once inside she stood with her back to the door letting it hold her up, for she knew her strength was all but gone. What had that woman done to her? It was as if an invisible hand reached inside her chest and tried to crush her heart and lungs. She gasped for air.

Zoey pulled out her iPad and opened it to a Google search. "There must be a place to rent in this town."

A voice drifted from the windows that surrounded the large window seat. Shapes and shadows that weren't quite distinguishable moved in the glass, whispers emanated between the window sills. "She won't let you go. No one leaves this room. Don't you know?"

The iPad fell out of her hand, panic gripped her heart. Her chest heaved in terror-filled breaths. Zoey's eyes searched back and forth frantically for someone or something rational. She rushed through the door into the hallway, all reason gone from her mind.

Naomi walked into the only other room on the top floor and closed the door behind her. Zoey chased after her and flung open the door.

"Naomi…" Zoey stood speechless for a moment. Naomi was not in the room. In fact, it wasn't much of a room at all, but a linen closet. She noticed the corner of a rusted metal toolbox sticking out from behind cleaning supplies on the bottom shelf.

She hesitated for a moment, and cautiously reached for it, pulling it open.

A voice whispered through the halls. "Look beneath. Set us free or join us." The last words ran down her back like frozen tentacles. Her eyes shot to an old claw hammer. She grabbed it and sprinted back to her room.

"Look beneath." She panted wildly as she saw the faded wool rug that covered the hardwood floor. She yanked back the rug. All her strength, her fury, and sanity surged through the tool as she dug at floor boards and pulled them up.

There it was. Zoey sat back out of breath, her heart pounding, sweat dripping down her brow. She gasped, and with eyes closed, turned her head away and wept. The claw hammer fell from her hand. She wiped her eyes and her brow, and forced herself to look back at the horror before her.

There, underneath the floor boards were bones. Human bones. Too many bones to count.

Faint cries filled the room followed by a loud crack. Zoey looked up at the window as it shattered. She could see faint shapes and colors as spirits twisted around flying out of the hidden casket that had imprisoned them and escaped through cracks in the glass.

Zoey got up and fumbled for the door knob behind her without taking her eyes off the window panes. In a movement faster than she thought possible, she grabbed her purse off the bed and raced downstairs and out the front door. She didn't stop running until she was three blocks away on Cypress Avenue. She continued walking north until she came to 5th Street. And there on the corner of 5th and Cypress sat a tiny cottage-style home with a for rent sign in the window. And on the front step, curled up in the doorway, was tom cat.

Zoey ran up to the house and laughed through her fear. Trapped souls were now free, and so was she.

Birth is not the beginning, and death is not the end.

A MEASURE OF GUILT

When someone behaves insanely, to help them heal, you must find the sanity in them.

Murder is cruel in any form, but to murder someone you love leaves an imprint on the soul. Tevi Richardson sat in her office at the Tillamook Mental Health clinic studying her research papers. Her eyes glazed over as she reread the pages again. She knew even here she would not find the one answer she was looking for, some reason, some explanation of why her brother, David, killed their father and then himself.

"She's coming for you." The voice said.

Tevi looked up startled. But no one was in the room with her.

"Who said that?" Even before she asked, she knew it was David. But he died 32 years ago. She shook her head. I've been working too long, she thought.

Her phone line buzzed, and the perky voice on the other end greeted her. "Miss Richardson, your two o'clock is here."

Tevi got up, looked in the mirror to make sure no hair had fallen out of her tidy bun, and her plain gray suit was neat and unwrinkled. She freshened her lipstick, one frivolity she allowed herself.

Lizzy sat in the lobby, staring mindlessly at colorful fish in the large aquarium. Tevi gestured toward her office. "Lizzy, good to see you. Right on time as always."

Lizzy looked up and tried to smile, but there was no sincerity behind the motion. She followed Tevi back to her office.

Shutting the door behind them, Tevi listened to Lizzy talk about her loss and her depression. The session was over and Tevi bid her client goodbye for another month. She walked out to the front desk in the lobby where Carol, the receptionist, sat texting on her cell phone.

Tevi cleared her throat. Carol didn't stop.

"Carol, I'm getting ready to leave for the day, and don't forget I'm going into Salem tomorrow and won't be in."

Carol nodded her acknowledgment, smiling at a text, and quickly sending a reply. Tevi walked out shaking her head in disapproval of the lack of professionalism.

"Mindless youth," she mumbled as she headed to the parking lot.

Tevi drove her Volvo around the bay to Garibaldi, to her lovely home on Acacia Avenue, two blocks from the shore. She had moved here only 18 months earlier from Phoenix, and a past she wanted no part of.

The following morning found Tevi on the long drive to Salem and the Oregon State Penitentiary. She was participating in a study for her dissertation, the measure of guilt found in those who murdered relatives and loved ones. The subject was personal for Tevi. As she drove, images from her youth flashed through her memory.

Despite all her training, despite all she'd learned, she still couldn't stop pictures of her past from invading her present. She wanted so much to forget the day she and her twin sister Terri witnessed death first hand. They were 14 years old. They hid in the closet, as they often did, to escape another family fight. And on a hot August evening, they watched through the slats of the closet door as their brother shot their father and then himself. Tevi became a grief counselor searching for understanding. Terri turned to alcoholism, barely living from bottle to bottle.

Arriving at the penitentiary and waiting at the gate while the guard checked her off the guest list, Tevi ran through her own checklist. She made sure to wear black, since they were told to never wear blue. Tevi did not have a large wardrobe, and she especially didn't have a colorful one. She made sure her clothes were loose fitting and not revealing. Her hair was pulled back and no jewelry. Her briefcase sat on the seat beside her.

"It's okay Miss Richardson, you can go on in." The guard stood back and the large metal gate opened, allowing her to drive through to the administration building. The complex was ominous, its massive stone walls standing stark against a pale gray sky.

Guard Phillips was young and tall, with square shoulders, a sharp jaw, and hair that was the worst comb-over she'd ever seen. He was pleasant enough around Tevi, but he gave the men no slack when herding them in like cattle to the class room. He seated the convicts in a semi-circle with George and Wes in the center and two other prisoners on either side of them.

Dr. Phillip Stone was working on the study with Tevi. He was already in the room with his notes in front of him. Tevi took her seat beside him and pulled her notes and papers out of her case. Guard Phillips stood behind them. She looked through her notes from the last session and then up at the men across from her.

George had been convicted of murdering his wife. He was slim and pale, a sad man with sunken eyes behind wire rim glasses. He seemed the least threatening of the group.

There was John, a large black man who was loud with a more aggressive personality; he murdered his wife as well.

Ryan was pudgy, bald, and covered with tattoos. He claimed his sister's death was an accident. They were fighting, and he didn't mean to push her out the window.

Wes was a tall skinny cowboy with a deep scar across his chin. He murdered his twin boys to keep from losing them in a nasty divorce battle, convinced his wife was in league with Satan.

A.J. murdered his brother, although he said it was justified.

Cliff had a round bald head, and one roaming eye. Cliff wrote his mother's rules on a pillow, then carefully placed the pillow over her while she slept and smothered her, the way she had smothered him. He felt it was poetic justice.

This was Tevi's tenth session with the men. The meetings had produced useful information for her research.

George was the one who confused her the most. The other men were generous with details, wanting to defend why they did what they did, showing it wasn't really their fault, thinking they were as much a victim as the ones they killed. But George rarely spoke up, his answers were brief, and he consistently maintained his innocence.

"George, where did your wife work?" Tevi questioned.

George rarely looked up. "She worked here. She was a nurse in the infirmary."

Dr. Stone and Tevi both scribbled on their notepads. She looked at George more closely. "Take me step by step, the last time you saw her, not just physically, but emotionally, what were you feeling?"

Ryan folded his arms over his chest and rocked back with a smirk. "He's gonna' tell you he didn't do it. How many times do we have to hear this dribble?"

Tevi prodded. "George, please."

George cleared his throat. "I had gone on a field trip to Newport with my class. We were late getting back. By the time I reached the house. Sally..." His voice quivered, his face hardened. He sat silent, remembering.

Dr. Stone spoke up. "Yes, George. We have the physical details, but what of the emotions?"

George didn't speak. He chewed on his lower lip.

Tevi looked at her notes. "We know Sally was..."

"Sally was lying on the bed, her blouse ripped, and...she had been shot once in the heart."

Ryan rolled his eyes. "Come on Doc. You already know he thinks he didn't do it." He looked over at George and winked. "Maybe the boogie man broke in and killed his wife. No wait, there was no sign of a break in." He tilted his chair back and laughed.

George frowned. "I couldn't breathe. My legs went limp; I fell to my knees on the floor beside the bed. I tried to shake her, but she just kept staring up at the ceiling." George looked straight at Tevi. "What did I feel? I felt like I was the one who had just died."

Tevi gave him time. He took a shaky breath, wiped his face and continued. "I tried to button her blouse back up, but the buttons were gone, I don't know where they went."

Dr. Stone pointed his pencil at George. "And then you called 9-1-1."

George continued. "That was the last time I saw her. I was sitting beside her, holding her in my arms when they came. And then they took me away. I didn't care anymore." He looked at Ryan. "My only guilt is that I wasn't there to protect her."

Tevi could see in George's eyes that he had given up.

Guard Phillips looked at the clock on the wall. "Okay girls, time to go back to your cells. Crying time is over." He walked through a door and ushered the men out of the room.

As the men filed out, Tevi heard David's voice behind her. "She's coming for you. She comes to save your life." She jerked her head around, but no one was there.

"David?"

"Who's David?" Dr. Stone asked.

"A haunting memory, nothing more."

Tevi and Dr. Stone walked out together. She looked at him as she signed out. "Dr. Stone, do you think there's any possibility that George is innocent?"

Dr. Stone was large and round and never looked her in the eye. "Of course not. They had ample evidence implicating him, and there was no trace of anyone else there. No break-in. Besides, if you read the police report, neighbors claimed she was cheating on him. He probably found her in bed with her lover, and in his jealous rage killed her. It's not uncommon."

"What about the lover?" she asked.

Dr. Stone held the door open for her to leave the building. "He probably got away. Or he's dead somewhere too, and they haven't found the body."

Tevi got to her car and watched Dr. Stone drive away in his large shiny black Mercedes. She glanced back and saw Guard Phillips walking across the lawn and called out. "Guard Phillips! Guard Phillips, can I talk to you?"

Guard Phillips walked over to Tevi and smiled. "Sure Dr. Richardson, what do you need?"

"I know this sounds crazy, but I feel there's a strong possibility George Ware could be innocent. What if he was framed? Maybe his wife was having an affair; maybe it was her lover who killed her?"

Guard Phillips tilted his head, looked at her over his dark sunglasses. "Don't you worry about things like that Doctor. I knew Sally Ware, and she was not cheating on George. It was all in his imagination. This guy's a real nut case, trust me." He smacked the gum in his mouth and smiled at Tevi. "They all want you to think they're innocent." He laughed as he walked back to the main building.

Tevi got in her Volvo and headed back to Garibaldi. A storm rolled in from the ocean. She could see it in the distance, dark clouds and a rumble of thunder. After an hour of driving, rain hit and she turned her wipers on. She couldn't stop thinking about George.

It was late when Tevi pulled into Garibaldi. She rounded the corner and hit the button for the garage door to open, and noticed someone sitting on her doorstep. She quickly pulled in and closed the garage, walking around to the front door.

Tevi stood there in amazement. "I don't believe it!"

Terri Richardson looked up at her twin sister and stretched her back, stood up and held out her arms. "You aren't going to give me a hug?"

Tevi was speechless. She didn't move.

Terri shrugged and brought her arms back down. "I guess not."

"What are you doing here?" Tevi's tone was cold with years of anger and resentment.

"Hey, I'm glad to see you too. I came to give you this." She took a crumpled piece of notebook paper out of her pocket and handed it to Tevi.

Tevi looked at it suspiciously. "You'd better come in before someone sees you." She opened the door and the two went inside. It wasn't the fact that Terri was disheveled, wearing torn jeans and a faded denim jacket with a low-cut red sweater. She didn't want her neighbors knowing she had a twin sister, especially an alcoholic one.

Terri looked around the immaculate house, and back at the crumpled note in Tevi's hand. "Aren't you going to read it?"

Tevi glanced at the paper in her fingers, the scribbled words, smeared and jumbled.

"You certainly were hard enough to find. I practically had to hire a detective."

Tevi sighed. "Maybe that's because I didn't want to be found."

"Yeah well, look Sis, I don't want to put you out. I just wanted to give you that."

Tevi rolled her shoulders. "I'm really tired; I've had a long day. How about we discuss this in the morning?" Tevi still clutched the handwritten note.

Terri smiled. "I'd like that, Sis. I'd like that a lot." There was sincerity in her voice that Tevi had not heard since they were children.

"You can stay in the guest room tonight."

Tevi sat in her bed with the lamp on and read the crumpled letter of apologies, smearing the words with her tears.

The storm was gone in the morning and the sun was shining over Garibaldi. Tevi got up to find her sister in the kitchen rummaging through cupboards. "What are you looking for?" Tevi asked. "I don't have any alcohol."

"Good morning to you too. I was hoping to find some coffee. I really need some caffeine!"

Tevi sighed. "Oh that's right, I'm out and I haven't made it to the store yet. Listen, I need to make a phone call and then we'll run down to the Parkside Coffee House and get something. You could take a shower and clean up a little first."

"I'm fine. How do you live in this place? It's so...so sanitary." Terri glanced at black and white scenic photographs on the wall. "No family pictures?"

Tevi dialed the phone and waited a moment. "Hello, yes, this is Miss Richardson. Is Warden Middleton in?...Thank you. Warden, I wanted to discuss some rather disturbing findings I've come up with regarding your inmate George Ware. I think it's quite possible he is not guilty of murdering his wife. Is there a way to look deeper into his case? Thank you, I appreciate it." She waited another moment then hung up the phone.

"What's that all about?" Terri asked.

"Oh, nothing really. Work. Anyway, I just can't help but believe that this man was framed for the murder of his wife."

Terri smirked. "Well that's not really 'nothing'!"

"I suppose you're right. Let's go get some coffee, I need it too."

Aiden was just finishing up an order for a couple when Tevi and Terri walked in. "Hi Miss Richardson. Whoa. There's two of you!"

Tevi looked embarassed. "I'll have my usual." She looked over at Terri as she pulled out her wallet. "What do you want?"

Terri read the large menu on the wall, her smile filled her face. "I'll have a skinny, mocha, double Vodka latte." She laughed and looked at Tevi, who was glaring at her. "Joking,

I'm only joking." She turned back to Aiden. "Make it a single!" She laughed again.

They walked out into the sun shine. The air was a pleasant 65 degrees. Tevi felt her sanity return as she drank the hot liquid in her cup. "That's what I needed. Listen Terri, I have some work I have to do, I'll drop you back off at the house and we can talk more over dinner this evening. I'm sure you'll be fine there."

"Sure." Terri grinned. "I'll make dinner for you."

Tevi looked skeptical. "Um, you don't cook. How about I bring pizza home."

"Pizza it is."

Tevi sat in her office at the clinic, looking at the figurine on her desk of Little Bo Peep crying over her lost sheep.

Carol brought in a phone message and handed it to her. Tevi wondered as she watched the young lady leave the room, how anyone could walk in such high heeled platform shoes without falling over or causing serious damage?

Tevi looked at the note. It was from Warden Middleton, and it simply stated he was questioning his staff who might have had any contact with Sally Ware, but if she wanted to take it further, she would need to contact the prosecuting attorney's office. Tevi sat back and huffed. "Innocent until proven guilty, my ass. More like guilty until proven innocent. There must be a way." She rummaged through the stack of papers on her desk.

Tevi had a tendency to work late hours, and today was no exception. She looked at her watch, it was half past seven. She needed to order a pizza. Tevi was surprised to find her sister still sober when she got home.

Tevi noticed the one-year-sober pin on Terri's jacket lapel. She nodded to the pin. "Where'd you steal that from?"

"I didn't steal it. I earned it."

Tevi looked skeptical. They spent the evening talking and eating pizza.

They were interrupted by a knock on the door. Tevi got up and opened it to find Mayme Divine. She ushered her in. "What's wrong?"

Mayme held tight to the leash in her hand connected to her corgi that stood next to her. She seemed frazzled and frightened. "Priscilla has disappeared. Elvis and I have been looking for her for hours and I can't find her. Elvis keeps coming to your yard. I thought maybe she came here?"

Terri put her pizza down. "Elvis is alive? I knew it!"

Tevi scowled at her sister. "Elvis and Priscilla are her dogs." She looked back to a worried Mayme. "Let me get my shoes on and I'll help you look."

Terri washed her hands at the sink and smiled at Tevi. "Listen sis, I'm beat, can I just take a hot shower and call it a night?"

Tevi pulled a jacket on. "Sure, you'll have to use my shower, the guest bathroom one leaks. I won't be long." She grabbed a flashlight from the coat closet and they were out the door.

Tevi and Mayme walked up and down the streets calling out for Priscilla. Elvis howled for his mate as well.

Mayme looked at Tevi. "I didn't know you had a sister. Come to think of it, I don't know anything about your family."

Tevi moved the flashlight back and forth. "Not much to talk about, pretty boring stuff really."

Mayme mused. "And yet you're a counselor whose job it is to talk to people about their lives, boring as they may be."

"My sister and I haven't been on the best of terms over the years. I just don't want to have to explain that to people, so I don't mention it at all."

"But she's your sister. And she looks exactly like you."

Elvis ran to a bush and started barking like crazy. "Priscilla, is that you?" Mayme dug into the brush and pulled out a scared, whimpering corgi. "Oh thank God, she's okay!" Mayme held Priscilla in her arms and hugged her like a long lost child. Elvis jumped trying to get to his rescued mate.

Mayme wiped some tears off her cheek and fastened a second leash to Priscilla's collar, and let the two dogs greet each other. She stood up, smiling through her tears. "I just don't know what I would have done if I lost her."

Tevi put an arm around Mayme and headed them back to her house. "I'm glad you found her and that she's safe."

As they neared Tevi's house, a small dark sedan squealed its tires and sped around the corner out of sight. Tevi's heart skipped a beat as she got closer to her house and noticed the front door ajar. She would never leave the door open. Something was wrong. She left Mayme on the sidewalk and ran to the house.

"Terri! Terri, are you still here?" Fear pulsed through her veins.

Tevi ran upstairs two steps at a time, her heart racing faster than her feet. The bathroom shower was running in her master suite with the shower door. Terri lay on the shower floor with her arm half out of the shower. Blood mingled with running water. A bullet hole pierced her chest directly over her heart.

Tevi gasped. She covered her mouth and walked backward until she hit the bed.

Mayme stood in the doorway and called out. "Tevi, is everything okay? You took off in such a hurry." She hooked the two dog leashes over the porch railing. "You two stay here, sit." Mayme walked upstairs.

Tevi heaved between sobs trying to catch a breath, her eyes so filled with tears she couldn't see, her heart so full of pain she couldn't speak. She grabbed the jacket from her bed and clutched the one-year-sober pin in her fingers as tight as she could. She would never let go, never again.

Mayme stood there taking in the sight, shaking her head. "Lord almighty!" She rushed over to the bed and scooped up Tevi in her arms and rocked her like a mother rocks a baby. It felt like an eternity had passed before Tevi quit crying, but Mayme didn't let go until she stopped.

"Who knew your sister was here?"

Tevi's voice cracked with pain. "No one. No one even knew I had a sister."

"Bless my soul. But that would mean…"

Tevi wiped her eyes with a Kleenex, and blew her nose. "What?"

"The killer thought she was you." Mayme said. "I'll call Ethan, he'll know what to do."

"Why would anyone want to kill me?"

Mayme shook her head. "I don't know."

Tevi got down on the floor, crawled over to her sister and held her hand.

Mayme turned the shower off, and pulled a sheet out of the linen closet and drew it over the wet body on the shower floor. Water and blood saturated the cloth.

Tevi didn't move. She stayed on the floor next to her sister.

Mayme pulled her cell phone out and punched a button from her speed dial. "Ethan, I'm at Tevi Richardson's, you need to get over here right away." Mayme took a blanket off the end of the bed and wrapped it around Tevi as she lay on the floor. "You just stay put. Ethan will take care of this." She headed downstairs.

Sheriff Ethan Johnson pulled up to the front of the house, the blue and red lights flashing on his pickup. He turned them off and headed to the front door. Mayme greeted him there and ushered him in quickly.

"You found your dog." He said.

"Yes, oh yes, Tevi helped me find her."

Ethan peered at the two dogs lying side by side on the porch. "I told you I'd help you search."

"I know, I know. But that's not what I called you about. When we got back to the house we discovered a murder."

Ethan instinctively put his hand over his pistol. "Murder?"

"Whoever did it is long gone now. But we do have a situation here."

Mayme led Ethan upstairs to the master bedroom and the two sisters. She explained the whole situation to him.

Ethan pulled out his cell phone and called the coroner. "This is Sheriff Johnson, I need you to come pick up a body."

Mayme paced. "We can release to the news that Tevi was found dead in her home. That will give you some time to find the murderer. Besides, if we let it out that Tevi is alive, her life could still be in danger."

"You've got a point." He knelt down to a solemn Tevi clasping her sister's hand. "Miss Richardson, is there a place you can stay until we get this figured out?"

Tevi didn't take her eyes off of her sister. "It was supposed to be me. He thought he killed me. He didn't even know her." She started crying again.

Mayme put her arm around Tevi's shoulder.

Tevi sniffed. "I didn't know she was coming. She just showed up."

Ethan looked down at the body on the floor. "She rode in on a wind of death."

Tevi's eyes got big as she looked up at Ethan. "What did you say?"

He shrugged. "It's just a saying."

Tevi sat up clutching her sister's jacket and the AA pin tight to her chest. "She's the one. She came for me." She shook her head as her chin quivered.

Mayme looked around the room. "Tell you what Ethan, how about if she stays with me. I've got that nice family room and guest room in the basement; she can hide in there for now."

"I can't leave my sister. I can't leave her."

"Dear, they'll have to take her body to the morgue. She can't stay here. Come home with me and they'll catch whoever did this. I promise." Mayme knelt down beside Tevi. Mayme grabbed Terri's clothes and handed them to Tevi. "You put these on. You and I'll sneak out your back door and over to my house, while they take Terri out the front door."

Mayme looked at Ethan. "Everyone will be watching you, and they won't notice us."

Tevi changed into Terri's faded jeans, sweatshirt and jacket. She pulled a stocking cap on her head, and left everything else behind.

The following day Tevi sat staring out the window in Mayme's kitchen. "Why did she have to come?" She watched the sheriff's pickup pull into the driveway. Ethan took his black cowboy hat off as he entered the house and nodded at Mayme and Tevi.

Mayme sat on the couch with Elvis and Priscilla at her feet. "Any news?"

Ethan rolled a toothpick from side to side in his mouth. "Word spread pretty fast that Tevi was shot dead in her home. We have the house taped off for now as a crime scene."

Tevi looked up at the tall sheriff. "She shouldn't have come."

Ethen walked over and kneeled down in front of her. "I will get your sister's killer, but you've got to give me a little to go on first. Like why someone would want to kill you?"

Tevi shrugged. "I don't know."

Ethan pulled out a small notepad from his shirt pocket. "Your office said you weren't working on anything significant. But maybe you had a client or patient that…"

Tevi's eyes got big. "George Ware. I was checking into his case."

"His case?"

"He's in the state pen for murdering his wife, but I uncovered information that suggested he was innocent."

Ethan stood up and put his hat back on. "Well that's a place for me to start. I'll talk to you two ladies soon." He nodded in their direction. "Miss Richardson, again I am so sorry that you have to go through this. But trust me, we are doing all we can."

"And what is that?" Her eyes were swollen and red from crying.

Ethan smiled at her. "Our best, ma'am."

Mayme pulled on a jacket over her heavy sweater. "I'll walk you out, Ethan." She grabbed the dog's leashes off the hook by the door. "Come on kids, let's go for a walk."

Elvis and Priscilla jumped and ran in excitement to the kitchen door.

Tevi waited and watched out the window Mayme and Ethan walk outside holding hands. She watched him steal a kiss from Mayme and drive away.

An hour later Mayme and the two corgis returned to find Tevi still sitting by the kitchen window. She was wearing Terri's jacket with the one-year-sober pin on the lapel.

Mayme closed the door and took the leashes off the dogs. "Are you okay dear?"

Tevi's head shook slowly. "I wish she had stayed away. She would still be alive if she hadn't come."

Mayme poured a cup of coffee and sat down. "Yes, but then you'd be the one dead."

Tevi looked up at Mayme. "George's wife's killer murdered Terri, thinking it was me."

"And by doing so, he protected his alibi, and George stays in prison, and he stays free."

Tevi sighed. "It should have been me. I feel like her death is on my hands."

"It's not your fault your sister got killed." Mayme sipped her coffee.

"It feels like it is."

Mayme looked out her window; she could see the ocean from here. "Where did George and his wife live before all this happened?"

"I don't know their exact address. It never came up."

"Let me do some digging. It's what I do best." Mayme said.

Tevi let out a sigh. "I suppose it's a good thing that you work for a newspaper then, huh?"

Mayme winked at her. "Life is divine that way." She handed Tevi the current copy of the small weekly newspaper.

"Here, you can catch up. But make sure you stay put. Don't leave the house. You have my cell number. If you need anything you call me, and only me. Everyone in town thinks you're dead."

Tevi glanced at the newspaper on the table. "For all practical purposes, I feel dead." She spent the day inside, reading the newspaper, staring out the window, petting Elvis and Priscilla, waiting to be alive again.

Mayme came back home after a few hours, scratching her head as she walked in the back door. She went downstairs and found Tevi asleep on the couch. She tried to tiptoe out of the room, but Tevi woke up.

"Mayme, did you find anything?"

Mayme smiled and walked over to a rocking chair and sat down.

"You know, I found a lot of things. This just keeps getting more and more interesting by the minute."

Tevi yawned and stretched. "How so?"

"I did some research at work, and Ethan went to your office to get your files on this study at the prison. Your secretary, Carol, gave him everything. She said no one had been in your office since you left it last. But there is nothing about George in your paperwork at all. According to what she gave Ethan, you were only working with five men at the prison, not six."

"Bitch!" Tevi said.

"Indeed." Mayme agreed. "Did you know George and Sally Ware lived kitty corner from your secretary?"

"So maybe Carol knows who the killer is?" Tevi's confusion was giving her a headache.

"This might even go deeper than we thought initially."

Mayme ran out on a few more errands, then came home in the early evening with a box. She handed the box to Tevi.

"Ethan wants you to put this on and wear it."

Tevi opened the box and pulled out the bulky vest. "For how long?"

"Oh, I think we'll know."

Mayme got up and fixed a nice steak dinner for herself and Tevi. The evening air had a mild chill to it, but it was fresh and inviting. Mayme poured them each a glass of red wine as they sat on the back deck and ate their steaks and drank their wine.

Tevi swallowed a generous bite of medium rare tenderloin. "What did you do today? Did you talk to the sheriff?"

Mayme turned the stereo up so they could hear the music outside. "Yes. And he had a plan." She took a sip of wine and leaned back. "Per his instructions, I went to your office and told your secretary that you were still alive, and hiding out at my place. Then I called Doctor Stone, and the Warden and told them the same. I explained what happened, and that we felt we had your sister's killer locked up safe."

Tevi almost choked on her beef. "You what? Are you crazy?"

Mayme looked around. "Well, my ex-husbands thought so. But I outsmarted all of them. I think we'll outsmart this fella too."

Just then, a subtle buzzing ripped through the air and hit Tevi in the middle of the chest. It knocked her back and she fell out of her chair on to the deck. Mayme smiled and ducked down. "Stay down dear, this is it!"

Sirens and shouting filled the air. Tevi and Mayme crawled into the house and out of harm's way.

"What's going on?" Tevi asked as she peeled the bullet-proof vest off.

"I suspect Ethan's plan worked. The news of your condition brought your sister's killer out to finish the job he started. I suggest we just lay low and let the men do their work. Elvis and Priscilla jumped on Mayme licking her face.

Tevi felt her chest where the bullet hit the vest. It was tender, but not hurt.

Twenty minutes later Sheriff Johnson came to the back door. "Mayme, you ladies okay?"

Mayme sat up with Elvis and Priscilla on her lap. "We are indeed."

Ethan walked in and offered a hand to help her up off the floor. "Seems Sally Ware was having an affair with someone, a someone named Carol."

Mayme reached down and helped Tevi up. She looked at the bullet-proof vest with a bullet lodged right over the heart. "Carol?"

Tevi shook her head. "It couldn't be. Carol?"

"Yes, Miss Richardson. My deputy just hauled her in to jail. Would you like me to take you home now?"

Tevi nodded and clutched the one-year-sober pin in her hand.

And in the end, we find the beginning.

MISTS OF GARIBALDI

DARK ART

She wants to live, yet wishes she were dead. She wants to laugh, but only cries.

Death clung to the winter wind that wailed across the bay into Garibaldi. Lizzy and Doug Yamamoto snuggled into bed, protecting each other from the coastal winter's chill.

Doug gasped for air. He grabbed the blankets with a fisted hand and held them to his chest. Pain seared through his words. "Lizzy, I can't…"

Lizzy knocked things off the night stand searching frantically for the phone. "Oh my God, honey, breathe!"

Fumbling through her tears, she dialed 911. "My husband can't breathe, please hurry!" She dropped the phone and put her mouth over his and blew into his lungs.

No breath came out of Doug's mouth. No life sparkled in his eyes, nor beat sounded in his heart.

Lizzy collapsed over him, sobbing.

After letting the emergency crew in, Lizzy sat in the corner of the room wrapped in a quilt cocoon, her knees pulled up tightly to her chest, her long black hair draped over her shoulders. She sobbed as she watched the paramedics take her husband away. Though her heart still beat, she felt as though her life ended with Doug's.

Lizzy huddled in the chair the rest of the night. She couldn't get back in the bed, not alone, not without him. The morning sun found her still in the chair, wrapped tight in the quilt. Doug was only 45. He was healthy and athletic. Now he was gone.

Days and nights were a blur to Lizzy. She was disconnected from life, the world floated around her in a surreal fashion. Her heart ached. Nothing made sense. Nothing mattered without Doug. A deep pit of loneliness had pulled her down and she didn't have the energy to climb out.

For weeks, friends stopped by daily to check on Lizzy and her oversized black and white cat, Buddha. Buddha was happy to see the people arrive and fill his dish with fresh food.

Lizzy tried to be sociable, but all she could think about was the darkness that was closing in on her. A heart attack one moment on a cold night changed her entire world. She watched her neighbors walk in and out, motions were a blur, sounds an echo. Nothing made sense anymore.

Lizzy sat in the glassed-in porch on the south side of her house. She watched the sun come up in the morning, and go down again at night, and small fishing vessels head out of the bay in hopes of large catches and calm seas. She watched the world, but did nothing to be a part of it.

Four months after Doug's passing, on a day the sun was shining, Lizzy stood in the kitchen, peering through the glass door that led to her art studio. She had not stepped in that room since Doug left. But now it invited her, the colors in the room seemed brilliant and alive. The sunlight glinted on jars and tubes of paint. She slowly reached out and opened the door. The heat from the room, with its solid glass wall, caressed her. She viewed her paintings stacked in the corner as if seeing old friends. Canvases and paints, brushes and sketch pads filled the small studio. A curio chest in the corner held her collection of antique brushes and art supplies.

Buddha brushed against her leg and jumped up on his favorite perch, a table next to the glass. She smiled at the cat. "Buddha, what do you see out there?" Buddha didn't answer, but watched the movement of birds in the sky hovering over the nearby rocky shore.

Lizzy walked around taking a mental inventory. "I suppose I should get back to painting one of these days, if I still remember how."

Buddha offered a "meow" of encouragement, and then took to bathing his short sleek fur.

Lizzy picked up a stack of papers and sifted through them. "Oh dear," she said, as she sat down in a chair at a small wooden desk to read through them more carefully. "I forgot all about Abigail's shop. I haven't taken any paintings to her in nearly a year. She must be furious with me."

Original watercolor paintings stood stacked against the wall with a burlap cover shielding them from the sunlight. Lizzy looked at her watch. "Buddha, I gotta run. Guard the place while I'm gone. I gotta go see the shrink so she can tell me how depressed I still am."

Lizzy petted the fat cat as he stretched out on his perch, purring with delight from the strokes. She picked him up to give him a hug, and grunted at his weight. "Buddha, for a fully enlightened being, you certainly are heavy. Might have to put your fat butt on a diet one of these days." The cat scowled at her, pinning his ears back.

Lizzy drove her small SUV around the bay and parked next to the Tillamook Mental Health clinic. She liked Tevi Richardson, her therapist; but wasn't convinced the visits were making a difference.

Dr. Richardson closed the door to her office and motioned for Lizzy to sit down in the comfortable overstuffed chair bathed in sunlight by the window. "Can I get you something to drink?"

"No thank you." Lizzy sighed.

Tevi opened her file and started a small digital recorder. She tilted her head and smiled at Lizzy, trying to get her to smile back. But Lizzy didn't smile. "Are you sleeping any better with the new prescription?"

Lizzy thought for a moment. "Some." She fixed her eyes on the small porcelain statue of Little Bo Peep crying over her lost sheep that sat on the edge of Tevi's desk. "Mostly I just wonder why I'm still here."

Tevi raised an eyebrow in curiosity. "What do you mean by that?"

Lizzy rolled her eyes. "It's just that with Doug gone, I can't find the purpose in my life anymore. Nothing seems to matter. If there is no meaning in life, why am I still here?"

Tevi collected her thoughts and folded her hands on her desk, looking Lizzy straight in the eye. "It's true the life you lived with Doug is gone, and the person you were at that time is gone with him. But you're a very talented and resourceful woman. I have no doubt that when you're ready, you will reach inside yourself and pull out the drive and focus you need to start over and move forward with your life."

Lizzy blinked her eyes and gave Tevi a doubtful look. "But what if I'm never ready? What if I don't ever find a direction or place to move forward to?"

Tevi wrote some notes down and leaned back in her high-backed leather chair. "Here's what I want you to do between now and our next visit. Write down three things you want to incorporate into your life. I want you to think about something you want to do, go on a trip, visit an old friend? Then tell me something you want to be, maybe take a college class, try a new career or hobby. Last think of an item you would like to get, some new furnishings, set of dishes, a new outfit? What are three things that you want in the next 30 days, the next six months, and the next year?"

Lizzy was intrigued. "So this is like my Aladdin's lamp? Three wishes?"

Tevi got up and walked around to the front of her desk. "Yes, exactly. Your life has a huge void without Doug, but you haven't figured out yet what to fill it with. Instead, you've been searching for answers as to why the loss. But loss doesn't necessarily have an answer, other than it is a mechanism to make room for something else. Go home and find the something else. Consider Aladdin's lamp rubbed, time to claim your life, your new life."

"Without Doug…"

Tevi led Lizzy to the door. "Yes, without Doug. Letting go doesn't mean forgetting. You will always carry his love in your heart. But you need to find something positive to focus on, instead of the loss. Find three things, Lizzy. But remember, they have to be specific. Generalizations like happiness don't work. Too vague. I look forward to our visit next week."

Lizzy left the clinic feeling a little better. As she drove out of Tillamook, she left the sun and drove into the cloud-covered greyness that hung over Garibaldi like a blanket. Her heart sank a little to see the sunshine had been replaced.

On her way home, Lizzy stopped on Garibaldi Avenue and parked in front of the Pirate's Plunder antique shop. Collectables filled shelves, tables and nooks. The glass counter in the front was filled with crystals, amethyst, and various other gem stones.

Abigail sat behind the glass counter, reading a dog-eared romance novel. She looked up from the pages and smiled while folding the corner of a page to mark her spot. She walked around the glass counter and hugged Lizzy. "Well I wondered if you were still around. How have you been my dear? I'm so sorry about Doug."

Lizzy smiled. "Thanks, Abbie. It's taking a while, but I'm starting to get around again."

"Did you bring me some new prints? The tourists love your watercolors."

Lizzy shook her head. She picked up a large crystal and marveled at it. "No, I'm sorry. I plan to start painting again though. I'll have some new prints for you soon." She set the crystal back down, walked around the store, and browsed, not looking for anything particular, but something she could put on her list for Tevi. She browsed through old books, jewelry, doilies, housewares, pillows, dishes and even a few clothing items. There didn't seem to be anything to stay for, and yet she couldn't leave. She felt there was something here she needed to find.

Lizzy walked to the front of the store again and looked at the jewelry, crystals and gems inside the glass case in front of Abigail.

Abigail put her book down next to an almost empty cup of tea. "Is there anything in particular you're looking for?"

Lizzy seemed lost for a moment and shrugged. "My therapist suggested I find three things I want in my life. But I can't think of three things I want." She pointed to the crystals. "Do they do anything? I mean, you know, have some kind of power or something?"

Abigail chuckled. "All stones have certain properties. I'm a personal believer that their properties can be utilized. But not everyone believes that."

Lizzy wrinkled her forehead. "What kind of properties? If I hold the crystal, will it lead me to what I need?"

Abigail came around the corner of the counter again, brushed the table next to her chair, knocked her tea cup over, and caught it before it fell to the floor. "It's not a divining rod, but a crystal will activate an energy center in your body. They're good for healing."

Lizzy pointed to a large grey and brown crystal. "What's that one?"

"The smoky quartz. It's best for warding off negative energies." Abigail picked up a medium sized rose quartz crystal and held it out to Lizzy. "Here, try this one."

Lizzy smiled as she held it, the pale pink stone gave her a sense of comfort. "I like this one. I'll take it. But I still need something else." She slowly turned around. "I need to get back to my art, but I think I want something different. Maybe instead of doing watercolors, I'll try oils for a while. Maybe even some different styles of painting, mix it up, you know?"

Abigail's eyes lit up. "Oh my gosh, why didn't I think of this? A couple of weeks ago I received some boxes from an estate sale in Salem. They claimed one of the brushes is an old Chinese brush somewhere between sixty and a hundred years old! Wait here, I'll go get it."

Abigail scooted off to the back of the store, and returned with a vintage artist's wood case. She sat it on the counter. Lizzy felt a surge of anticipation as the case was opened and they went through the items inside. Mostly it was normal art supplies, pallet knives, brushes and some nearly empty tubes of paint.

Lizzy picked up the well-used brushes and admired them. "These are excellent brushes, and they've been well taken care of. A Delta 270, a Mussini and a number eight Lyon Bristle Artist." She rummaged through the knives. "Loew Cornell and Japan. What a handsome collection." She rotated the knives and brushes one by one, each wood handle dark with age and stained with layers of paint.

Abigail took out an frayed silk bag that was under the tray in the box, and pulled a most unusual paint brush out of it. She held it up for inspection.

Lizzy was immediately drawn to the Chinese paint brush. "I've never seen anything like this. Yes, it must be at least a hundred years old." The handle was bamboo, with an animal hair brush on one end, and a bone hook at the other end. It captivated her. "How much?"

Abigail picked up her record books and thumbed through the pages. "The auctioneer said I was stealing this, only because no one there knew what it was worth. I'll give it to you for five hundred for the whole kit. But I dare say you could probably get five hundred just for that one brush." Abigail eyed it again over the top of her glasses.

Lizzy slipped the ancient brush back into its silk bag. "Deal. Check okay?"

Abigail laughed. "Only because it's you. I don't take checks from tourists anymore. Been stiffed too many times." She rang up the sale on the old cash register.

Lizzy smiled the whole time she wrote out the check. Excitement pulsed through her veins like an electrical surge.

A storm was rolling in from the ocean. It started with a light drizzle. By the time Lizzy drove up 10th and arrived at her home on Birch, the drizzle turned into a fierce rain.

Lizzy pulled into the carport and rushed into the house to start a fire in the fireplace. For the rest of that day and deep into the night, she sat on the floor of her studio sorting through her new treasures. The vintage artist case sat next to her, its contents laid out on a paint-spattered square of burlap. While inspecting the pieces, she wrote in her journal by the light of the flames that danced in the fireplace, and the moon that hung like a giant glowing orb above a black ocean. *Short, medium, and long range goals. Three things. How do I fill a void, a scary darkness that's consumed my life? I don't want to be afraid of the dark anymore.*

Lizzy looked up at Buddha as he inched his way closer to the fireplace, and finally lay down, stretching and yawning. "I want to paint differently, you know Buddha? Not the expected seascapes and light houses, but unusual paintings, unique and different." Buddha didn't seem to care.

Lizzy picked up the silk bag and slid the Chinese paint brush out. "This brush has stories to tell, and I want to tell them." She cradled the brush in her left hand as she continued writing. She looked over at Buddha again, who had closed his eyes and fallen asleep.

At the top of a fresh page she wrote *I want change. My three goals,* and numbered them.

One – reinvent myself through my art, take my painting to a whole new level and style.

Two – travel to distant and exotic places like Hong Kong and Singapore.

And three, she stopped and stared at the page. She wanted to say a new love. It was too much like saying it was okay that

Doug was gone. And it wasn't okay. She was still angry at him for leaving her.

Three – when the time is right, to fall in love again. She slowly closed the journal. Her path was set.

Lizzy lay in bed the following morning watching patches of clouds float by, and listened to gulls chattering outside her window. She got up and showered, then marveled at the tingle in her skin as she dried off. Something was different, very different. She wiped the steam off the bathroom mirror and stared at her reflection.

Had Lizzy changed so much from grief that she was not even recognizable to her own self? She turned sideways and noticed she was thin. When did this happen? She wondered. She didn't realize she had lost weight. Shoulders back, chest out, stomach in. Damn, she had never looked this good!

Lizzy spent the entire winter painting. No more light-houses and gentle sea shores. Her canvases became larger, her colors richer, and her images possessed with a hint of malevolence. Her art was spell-binding, drawing the innocent viewer into a murky place of darkness and uncertainty. She painted non-stop. Her hand had a will of its own, and moved from paint to canvas with artistic skills she never knew she had. Each canvas was more intense than the one before. Her strokes were large and fast, filled with fury, fire, and a pulsing drive from hand to brush.

By late summer, her work had completely transformed into frightening, obscure paintings, with a touch of evil the local shop and gallery owners were uncomfortable with. Even Abigail shook her head, "Bring back some pretty landscapes for me, Lizzy. Those I can sell."

Lizzy packed up her paintings and drove to Portland, to give a cutting-edge gallery there, a try. The curator seemed unsure at first, but when he laid eyes on her work he was immediately captured by it.

"How many pieces do you have?" He asked.

"I have a dozen in the car right now. You're more than welcome to pick out the ones you like." Lizzy held her breath while he walked around the large painting she had placed on the easel in his office. "Or if there's something different you'd like, I could…"

"No, no." He waved his hands, immersed in the painting. "Bring it in, bring it all in now. Let me see every piece."

Lizzy bounced with excitement. She was overwhelmed with gratitude to the force that had come into her life, as she loaded the paintings onto a cart and wheeled them into the gallery.

The curator bought all but two, and asked her to bring more as soon as she could.

Through connections and publicity of the Portland collection, Lizzy expanded to Seattle, Los Angeles and San Francisco. Even New York galleries were calling for her work. Lizzy Yamamoto had become the buzz of the occult art world.

The presence of fall had come early in September. Lizzy sat on her large deck overlooking the bay, sipping her coffee, and going through mail.

A current issue of *OCCULT* magazine was the first piece she picked up from the pile. Lizzy was on the cover standing between two large easels displaying her latest paintings. As an artist she was on fire, an overnight success. She soaked up the glory of her new standing, and the levels of attainment it brought.

Clothed in a long, deep purple robe, with a slinky gown on underneath, her long hair was unmanageable waves flying in the wind. Her blood pulsed through her veins like electric current.

"I look amazing. I am amazing!" Her words reverberated the length of her body in an orgasmic explosion.

Lizzy retreated indoors. All the shades and curtains were drawn, and the shadows soothed her. She stood in front of a large mirror in the hallway to admire her beauty. She thought of nothing but her art and success.

Lizzy's fame in the world of dark art consumed her entire life every waking moment. The curator in Los Angeles, who purchased the bulk of Lizzy's work, sent an agent, Dean, to handle her business.

Dean drove from California in mid-October to explain their relationship to Lizzy and review the contract that bound them to each other. He was sleek, with black hair, a goatee, a large diamond stud in his left ear, and deep green eyes. When he swooped in to Lizzy's home, Buddha hunched his back, hissed, and ran outside. The world seemed to shudder with each step he took. Lizzy went blank to his gaze and limp to his touch. With the wave of a hand, her body followed his motion. She was under his spell.

Dean stayed three days in Garibaldi, and on the third night, under a full moon, he kissed Lizzy goodbye and drove off.

Nothing could stop her now. Lizzy realized as the taillights disappeared onto 10th street. She was invincible. She had it all - beauty, talent, wealth, and the power to get more.

Lizzy let out a hideous laugh as she headed for her studio.

In late December Lizzy stepped on Buddha's squeaky toy. She stopped and looked down at the small rubber mouse. She couldn't place what it was, or why it was there. She should know why this toy was here, but she didn't. A dark mist clouded her mind and blocked out everything that did not serve the purpose of her art.

Walking past a mirror on the wall, Lizzy was startled by a glimpse of herself. It wasn't her reflection. This woman in the mirror's hair hung in thick tangled masses, with spiders nesting in their weaves. "I hate spiders." Lizzy recalled. But the woman in the reflection dismissed her claim and smiled.

Lizzy felt her heart race. She had not embraced the dark that frightened. Rather the darkness embraced her, surrounded her, engulfed her.

Lizzy ran to the kitchen looking under the table and in the corners of the room. "Buddha! Buddha, where are you?" His dishes were dusty and covered with fine cobwebs. When had she seen him last? She couldn't remember. She looked down at her hands. Her fingers were calloused and stained, with paint. Her nails were long and pointed.

Lizzy ran out the door and down to the beach. "Buddha!" she cried out. She rubbed frantically at her skin as if it were a layer of plastic she could peel off. She sat down on a large boulder and sobbed.

The chill of the ocean air was gone, the sound of the slapping waves had ceased. Lizzy looked up. She was no longer sitting on the rock, but in her studio, in front of a canvas waiting for her strokes. She watched her fingers grasp a paint brush and pull her hand to the canvas. She satisfied its bidding, black, deep purples, greens and blood reds filled the work. It was beautiful and terrifying.

Lizzy painted through the night and stopped as the sun began to crest over the horizon. She dropped the paint brush from her fingers and slowly backed away from the easel. She grabbed the Chinese brush out of the curio cabinet and slid it into its silk bag. She dropped the silk bag into a box of old newspapers waiting to be recycled, then pushed against the unseen force that trapped her in the room. It took all the strength she could muster to step through the door and drag herself upstairs. She was out of breath when she reached the top step and dropped to her knees.

She crawled to her bedroom, pulled the journal off the nightstand and lay on the floor flipping through the pages. Lizzy found it, the page where she had written her three wishes. She took the pen in the pocket of the book cover and crossed out the first two. Below them she scribbled 'I want my life back.' Lizzy dropped the journal on the floor. Unable to move, and barely able to breathe, she splayed across the carpet. Was this a dream? Everything went black.

In the glow of moonlight, Lizzy ran through cobblestone streets lined with narrow buildings. The town was empty. Faces peeked out windows, then darted from view. She pushed her way into a house. An old man and woman huddled into the dim corner, clasping each other for protection.

"I won't hurt you," she whispered to them. "Please help me find my way." But neither spoke, they hid their faces and looked the other way.

Light shone from underneath a door and spilled across the floor. Lizzy followed it and turned the gold doorknob. Doug stood in the center of a room of pure light. He held out his hand to her. "Return to my love, Lizzy. It will show you the way."

Lizzy woke in a panting sweat on the bedroom floor. She pulled herself to her feet, stumbled down the stairs, and rushed out the front door. She walked until she reached the antique shop at the center of town. She sat on the bench in front of the store and caught her breath.

Abigail entered the store from the rear, turned the lights on, flipped the closed sign around to open, and unlocked the front door. Lizzy heard the latch turn and rose to enter. By the time she reached the door, Abigail was heading for the counter. Lizzy reached for the door handle and the lock latched. She peered through the window. Abigail poured her morning tea and prepared to sit down behind the counter with a book in hand.

Abigail looked up and dropped her book to the floor. The store windows were enveloped in dark, murky colors, swirling like puddles of oil and water, looking for a way to get in. The fluid pushed and heaved against the old wood window frames, joints began to bow at its pressure. Lizzy clung in the center of the darkness, screaming for her release and begging for help.

"It's evil, Abbie. Please!"

Abigail grabbed her largest smoky quartz crystal and walked around the counter to stand in front of the door. She held the quartz up and spoke to the malicious entity outside her shop. "You are not welcome here and you will not enter. I banish you to the depths from which you rose, and you will never cross the threshold of this space, or enter Lizzy's being again."

Shrieks and unearthly screeching of metal raged through the air, but Abigail stood fast. The swirling fluid peeled from the shop and was pulled into the cracks of the earth.

The latch released and the door slowly creaked open. Abigail cautiously poked her head outside, thrusting the crystal in front of her. She looked down the sidewalk and saw Lizzy lying unconscious in front of the pharmacy, two shops over.

"Oh dear Lord!" Abigail gasped as she ran to Lizzy. She put her hand on Lizzy's neck and felt a faint pulse. She dug in her pocket for her cell phone and dialed 911. "I'm in front of the Garibaldi pharmacy; a woman is unconscious and barely breathing, please hurry." She slid her phone in her pocket and sat beside her young friend. Abigail placed Lizzy's head in her lap, and stroked her hair as she hummed a soft melody, waiting for the sirens to arrive.

Within minutes, EMTs rushed from an ambulance, lifted Lizzy's seemingly lifeless body off the sidewalk, and whisked her away to the hospital. Abigail watched as the lights flashed down the highway and around the bay.

Lizzy rested in her hospital room. A doctor came in, glanced at the chart beside her bed then looked at her. "Mrs. Yamamoto, I'm Dr. Roberts. How are you feeling?"

Lizzy's eyes fluttered and she smiled. "Tired, but good."

Dr. Roberts made a note on the chart. "You were severely dehydrated, which caused you to faint. Your blood sugar was low as well. Get more electrolytes in your system and you'll be fine. Do you have any other symptoms I should be aware of?"

Lizzy was so weak it took all her effort to manage a smile. "Thank you, Dr. Roberts. I'll be fine."

The physician noted her report on her chart and left the room.

A nurse came, check the IV drip and placed some items in a small brown paper bag. "Dr. Roberts has samples here of some additional supplements he want you to take with you. They'll help you get back on your feet a little quicker. You got a ride home, hon?"

Lizzy smiled. "Yes, I'll call a friend." She picked up the phone next to her bed and dialed. "Abbie? I'm at the hospital; can you come pick me up?"

An hour later Abigail showed up as Lizzy was signing discharge paperwork. She walked Lizzy out to the car and helped her in.

"So what did the doctor say?" Abigail asked, as she settled in behind the wheel.

Lizzy buckled her seat belt and took a deep breath. "He said I was dehydrated and my blood sugar was low. So they filled me back up and gave me some more vitamins to take. It's so weird. I feel like I just woke up from a coma." She laid her head back against the headrest. "I don't even know how I got here." Lizzy's eyes opened wide as she jerked her head around to look at Abigail. "Buddha, have you seen Buddha? Where's my kitty?" She said panicked.

"He's at the store." Abigail said reassuringly. "We can stop and pick him up on the way."

Lizzy closed her eyes, dropped her head back on the seat and smiled.

Abigail parked behind the antique shop and helped Lizzy into the store. She sat her down in an antique rocker and gave her a cup of tea. Lizzy gulped the warm Oolong. Abigail laughed. "Slow down dear, there's plenty more where that came from."

Lizzy smiled. "Thanks Abbie. Where's my Buddha?" she asked, in the form of a call. A meow came from the back of the store, and Buddha strolled up through the aisle and rubbed against her leg. She put the tea cup down, picked up her cat, and hugged him. "Buddha, I've missed you so much."

Abigail sat in her chair and looked over the rim of her glasses at Lizzy. "He showed up on my doorstep about a month ago. So I kept him here, out of harm's way."

Lizzy petted her cat as he curled up in a large ball on her lap and purred. "I don't know where I was Abbie. It's like a terrifying dream held me captive. I lost all track of time, and myself."

"Well you're found now. That's what counts."

Lizzy held snuggled Buddha and smiled. "I felt as if I was trapped inside a dark shadow, and no one could see me."

Abigail thought for a moment. "I always felt you underestimated your own strength."

Lizzy furrowed her brow. "My strength?"

"You were trapped. By what, I don't know."

Lizzy tilted her head as she thought about it, gazing about the many antiques in the small shop. "Can a paint brush have powers?"

"Everything has energy. It's not really power, but you were in such a vulnerable state after Doug died, I think a dark energy could have taken over." Abigail sipped her tea. "The important thing is that you escaped it yourself."

"I do feel like I've awakened from a deep sleep. And while I miss Doug again, it feels different now. I have this strange feeling that he's watching over me. Like he's guiding me to a new phase of my life. He always said life was an adventure."

Abigail got up and filled both of their tea cups again. "Oh, how delightful, I always love a good adventure. What will it be this time?"

Lizzy smiled. "I think I'll raise some money for the American Heart Association, and take up pottery."

The brass bell chimed as the shop door opened and a handsome, fair-skinned man in his early 40s walked in. He had the clearest gray eyes Lizzy had ever seen. She smiled and felt herself blush. When the time is right, she thought.

To be born again is simply to let go of the past.

DRAGON'S EYE

You have the vision now to look past all illusions.

The young man stood in the alley behind the Pirate's Plunder antique store, clutching the box that warmed and throbbed like a beating heart. He rushed around the corner, into the shop, and slid the box onto the counter.

Abigail St. George sat behind the glass counter reading a mystery novel with half the front cover torn off. Her gray hair was short and in no particular style, but seemed to shift depending on which way you looked at it. Vintage cat-eye glasses accented with small rhinestones, surrounded her soft gray eyes.

She flipped the page.

"Hey!" The man screeched, his eyes darting toward the windows. "How much will you give me for these things?" He never once glanced down at the box or Abigail, but kept his focus on the window.

Abigail glanced up at the young man and frowned. He was sloppy with jeans riding low on his hips, and dark stringy hair hanging across his face. But Abigail was always interested in finding new treasures. Her curiosity took over as she stood and pulled the box close. "What do you have, Bo?"

The young man looked bewildered. "How did you know my name?"

Abigail smirked, "I just read the tattoo on your neck. So what's in the box?"

"Old stuff, you know. A twenty and it's yours, lady."

Abigail opened the box. It was filled with mostly junk, books, a glass vase, a few worn silver-plated spoons, a china dinner plate, and a Waterford crystal wine glass, but only one.

She reached in the cash register drawer and held up a crisp ten dollar bill. "How about a ten?"

Bo snatched it from her fingers and was gone.

Abigail carefully pulled the items out of the box, wiped each one off with an old dish towel, and then gently placed it on the glass countertop. On closer inspection, the items proved more sellable, but less valuable than she hoped, and she was glad the young man took the $10 rather than the $20 she would have paid.

"What have we here?" She wondered, while pulling out a faded red velvet cube with worn corners, embossed with an oriental symbol. "Hiding at the bottom, eh?" She opened it to find a delicate bone china tea cup.

Abigail lifted the cup, examining the intricate hand-painted dragon that wrapped around the cup. The brilliant gold scales of the dragon reflected in her eyes. The inside of the cup was tea stained white. She sat down in her chair holding the new treasure in her hands.

Abigail lifted the cup up to the light. An eye painted into the china appeared in the bottom of the cup.

A dragon's eye.

Abigail gulped and cautiously returned the cup to its form-fitting box, and eased the box into the tote bag next to her chair. She logged the other items into her book, filled out price tags, and placed them on display, continually glancing over her shoulder at the bag.

At six o'clock Abigail turned the open sign in the window to closed, locked the front door and emptied the till, just as she had every night for the past eight years. Turning off the lights, she grabbed her tote bag and headed toward the back of the store. She climbed the narrow stairs to the small apartment above. The dreary rain outside her window made her shiver.

Abigail's apartment was filled with antiques from the shop below. Paintings and photographs covered the walls in no particular theme or pattern. Every time she found something she liked, she grabbed a hammer and nail and hung it wherever it would fit.

Settling in for the evening, Abigail sat by the window that gave her a perfect view of Garibaldi's bay, the jetty and the ocean beyond. She pulled a soft blanket over her legs and sipped a hot cup of Oolong tea.

Abigail pulled the paperback from her tote bag– a favorite she had read twice before. To avoid missing anything in town, she glanced out her window each time she turned a page. As she looked up between pages 45 and 46, she caught a glimmer of gold just past the jetty.

Abigail carefully bent the corner of the page, set the book down, and reached for her binoculars resting on the window's ledge. She scanned the bay and around the jetty, but didn't see…wait, there it was again. An iridescent creature leapt up from the water then sank down below the surface. Abigail refocused her binoculars to get a better look.

The rain fell harder obstructing her view.

A rustling sound in her tote bag startled her. Abigail slowly set the binoculars aside. The red velvet cube glowed, and then faded out. She trembled as she reached for the box, opened it, and lifted the cup from its nest. The dragon was gone.

She furrowed her brow, turning the cup around. There was no design or color at all. "I was sure it had a dragon on it, a gold filigree dragon." She held the cup up to the window, turning it on its side to peer through the bottom, and again, she gasped as the dragon's eye appeared, translucent within the china. The eye stared at her. She quickly returned the cup to the box and shoved it to the back corner of the book shelf against the wall. She grabbed her inhaler from the table beside her, shook it, and drew a deep breath. She turned back to the window, and clasped her hand over her mouth. Her eyes grew as the spine of the sea monster rose up and fell down through the waves near the jetty. His movement was a graceful dance with the tide. "What have I unleashed?" she whispered.

An hour passed before Abigail tore her gaze from the window. Her tea was cold and she had forgotten about dinner. She tried to read but gave up, unable to concentrate. Words of a novel were no match for the real story emerging from the bay. She picked up her binoculars and stared out the window again. It was too dark to see anything now, and it was time to get ready for bed. She checked the lock and deadbolt on her door, tugged to make sure they were latched, and pulled the privacy chain into its clasp.

Abigail tossed and turned in her sleep, dreaming of a large golden dragon awakened in the bay. He slithered across the rocks of the jetty, dove under the waves, and leapt into the air with a wing span as wide as the town.

The morning sun sifted through the blinds of the small one-bedroom apartment and landed on Abigail's eyelids. Curled in a ball with her blankets twisted around her, she opened one eye to look at the clock beside her bed. It was nearly seven o'clock, and time to get up. She winced as she stretched the night's aches out of her tight muscles, slid her feet into slippers and headed for her kitchenette.

Abigail glanced at the red box peeking at her from the book shelf, as she put her tea pot on the stove burner. She wanted to check the cup again; surely the dragon had only been a dream. As the water boiled she pulled the box out. Opening it slowly, her heart raced as she looked at the plain white cup within.

No dragon, no delicate gold leaf painting. Abigail pushed the lid onto the box, placed it back on the shelf and rearranged some books to hide it from her view.

The large windows of the shop were full of light on this sunny morning. The store was a treasure trove housing artwork, old music albums, clothes, furniture, toys and books. Abigail got to work readying it for the day. She swept the wood floors and ran a feather duster over surfaces. In the room dedicated to kitchen and dining items, she rearranged the new dishes and silver, then stood back to get a good view.

A ray of sunlight hit the corner of a crystal goblet on the table and bounced up into Abigail's eye. She saw a flash of gold and the view in front of her was replaced. How strange, Abigail thought. She was standing in her shop, yet it wasn't what she was seeing. She watched people move around a dimly lit bar, laughing and drinking. She sniffed the air embodied with beer, cigarette smoke, and odors of sweat and cheap cologne. She was consumed with the need to find someone who had taken something from her.

The scanning stopped with two young men sitting at a table beside the dart board on the wall. Bo drank a glass of beer, laughing. The young man with him was fair skinned, stalky with his hair stuffed under a biker skull cap. Hovering in the dark shadows of the high corners of the ceiling, her vision zoomed in closer. She saw his tattoo, his baggy pants, but no box.

The men bragged of their stolen bounty, laughed at their victims, and celebrated the money they made. They plotted their next heist and the cash it would bring.

After two hours and a dozen beers between them, the two got up and walked out the back door into the alley. A monstrous screech caused the two to cover their ears. A glint of gold reflected in their terror-filled eyes. They screamed and ran in opposite directions.

Bo ran around the corner and was gone. His friend with the skull cap fell, scrambled to his feet and tried to run again. Giant talons snatched him up and flung him against the brick building like a net full of fish. His body slid to the ground. The monstrous claws ripped his chest open, plunged in, and yanked out his heart.

Steam rose into the cold night as blood from severed veins seeped across his chest and drained onto the gravel. The beast hurled the dripping body into the dumpster behind the bar.

Then Abigail's vision soared upward as the town below her grew small. She reveled in the clear night sky, dotted with stars and bathed in the moon.

Abigail plopped into the chair behind her. The vision was so real, like she had stood over the young man, and felt the warmth of his blood on her hands. A chill cloaked her. She rushed to her chair behind the counter, grabbed her sweater and pulled it on as she dialed the sheriff's office. "Sally? This is Abigail St. George in Garibaldi. Is Sheriff Johnson in?"

"He's on the road right now. What's up?"

"I need him to check something out."

"If it's urgent, I can radio him. Is it urgent, Abigail?"

Abigail let out a whimper. "Maybe? I mean, yes, of course. I think a young man's been murdered. That's urgent, isn't it?"

"Murdered? Who? Where?"

Abigail hesitated. "I don't know. I just need to talk to Ethan. Please get him here quick."

Abigail tried to gulp down the ball of fear lodged in her throat, but it wouldn't budge. Worry filled her eyes as she disconnected the call.

In ten minutes the brass bell above the front door chimed when Sheriff Ethan Johnson barreled in. He was a fit man in his late 50s, with salt and pepper hair that peeked out from under a black cowboy hat. He pulled the hat off and ran his fingers through his wavy hair. "Abigail, what's this I hear about a murder?" The intensity of his stare was nearly painful.

Abigail shrugged and dropped her gaze to the shiny toes of Sheriff Johnson's cowboy boots. She bit her lip. "I don't know how to say this Ethan, without sounding crazy."

Ethan sat his cowboy hat on the counter, pulled a toothpick out of his shirt pocket, and stuck it in his mouth. "Then sound crazy. You know me. I'll just listen." He leaned back against the counter and comfortably crossed his arms.

Abigail described the bizarre events from the beginning as she paced, waving her hands to help the story free itself. "Then he took the money and just skedaddled out without even getting a receipt. These rash kids today."

"Is he the one murdered? Where's the body, Abigail?"

"I'm getting to that, just let me explain. He and his buddy were in a bar."

"What bar?"

"I don't know what bar. One with a dumpster in the alley. Maybe the Ghost Hole? Or one in Tillamook? But they stole all these items and they sold them."

"Did they steal from you? Was it a break in? You killed a burglar?"

"I didn't kill him. They didn't steal from me. But they sold me stolen items. I didn't know it at the time."

"Abigail, I can see you're rattled dear, so just slow down and tell me where the body is."

"I'm getting to that."

Ethan took a deep breath and nodded. "Okay, how do you know the items were stolen?"

"Because they were talking about it in the bar."

"So let me get this straight, you know these boys were selling stolen goods because you heard them talk about it in the bar, but you don't know if it was the bar across the street or ten miles away?"

Abigail nodded. "Right."

Ethan nearly bit the toothpick in half. "How could you go to a bar and not know where you were, Abby?

"This is the part that sounds a little crazy. The dragon took me, or showed me, anyway."

"What dragon?"

"The one that was on the cup he brought in."

"Abigail, I'd say you have crazy nailed down." He rolled the toothpick back and forth across his tongue. "You will get to the dead body soon, right?"

Abigail nodded. "I think one of them is dead in the dumpster."

Sheriff Johnson narrowed his eyes at her. "The dumpster behind the bar."

"Right." Abigail confirmed.

"Did you happen to see who the killer was?"

"It's hard to say, my angle of view was a little obscure."

"Okay Abigail, can you tell me anything that will help me find these guys? Did they mention anything at the bar about where they live, work, family?"

"No. But I know the one that came in here had a tattoo on his neck with his name Bo. I'd say they're in their early twenties. You know the type, their pants falling down, greasy hair; they drink and smoke, and steal." She emphasized the word 'steal'.

Ethan Johnson pulled the toothpick out of his mouth. "Abigail, you know as well as I do, you can't go making accusations like that without some kind of proof."

Abigail huffed in defensiveness. "I saw and heard the proof, Sheriff. They've been stealing. Check the pawn shops. But first please, check the dumpsters!"

"Okay, Abby, when did you see this happen?"

"This morning while I was getting ready to open. But in the vision, it was night. I saw the full moon."

Ethan rubbed his chin. "Vision, huh? Been adding something to your tea?" A teasing smirk broke across his face. Abigail glared at him.

"Okay, Abigail. I'll check out the dumpsters, in fact I'll get Charlie on it right away." Ethan picked his hat up from the counter and set it on his head. It was time to go prove Abigail St. George had just had a bad dream.

"Thank you, Ethan."

"Anytime, Abigail."

Abigail attempted to smile as Ethan waved while getting into his pickup. A queasiness swirled in her gut. It wasn't just a dream.

Abigail spent the rest of the day alphabetizing VHS movies, sorting through records and books, grouping them by genre. She folded table cloths and curtains.

Around four o'clock, she decided to wash her display windows. She pulled everything out of one, climbed in and sprayed the cleaner back and forth. A combination chair and step ladder helped her reach the high corners of the windows. She wiped the glass in circles, starting small then getting bigger. The symmetry of the circular motion restored order to her world. She smiled.

The bell on the door of the antique shop chimed. Abigail got off the stepladder. "Lizzy, it's so good to see you."

Lizzy Yamamoto set a box of pottery on the counter. "What do you think of these? I put a seashell motif on the items to appeal to tourists. I'm enjoying pottery so much more." She giggled with delight as she pulled a set of mugs out of the box.

Abigail walked behind the counter and looked at the pieces. "They're lovely. I'm so glad you came by. Say, I have a unique china tea cup that …" Her mouth froze unable to utter another syllable. She closed her mouth and caught her breath.

"Abby, are you all right? You look a little pale."

Abigail looked up into Lizzy's black eyes and forced a feeble smile. "No, no, I'm just a little overworked lately." She looked around the room, distracted, confused.

"Abby, I'm worried about you. Let me help."

"It's fine. The pottery looks great. I'll log it all in later, if that's okay?"

Lizzy smiled and reached across the counter putting her hand on Abigail's. "All right, I'm heading to Tillamook and Lincoln City. But if you need anything, you call my cell. Promise?"

Abigail nodded and smiled as Lizzy left.

With no customers all day, Abigail huffed out loud, "Enough." She locked the front door, turned the open sign around and headed up stairs.

"I have to destroy it; I have to get rid of that cup." As the words left her mouth, fear filled her mind. Abigail opened a small cupboard in her kitchenette and pulled a bottle of brandy from the back. She blew the dust off the lid and poured some in a glass. She gulped the nerve-settling liquid then poured a second round. She sat in her chair by the window, pulled the afghan over her lap, closed her eyes, and finished the rest of the brandy. Abigail tilted her face to the window and fell asleep.

Abigail watched the room light up with her standing in the center of a ball of flames. She jerked up her arm and shielded her eyes. A voice low and rough echoed inside her head. "Destroy it and you destroy yourself. My heart must be restored to its rightful place."

A truck on the street below honked its horn at a pedestrian. Abigail lunged forward in her chair, rubbed her eyes, and realized she had been dreaming. She tried, but couldn't keep her mind off the red box on the shelf. She wracked her brain for ways to protect the cup, but not keep the cup. She glanced down at the shelf. At least I can store it away from me, she thought.

She opened the shop and put the tea cup in the back corner of the bottom shelf of a cupboard behind the counter, where it would remain safe, and most importantly, out of sight. The evening was uneventful as she watched a couple of movies on TV then fell asleep reading a Nora Roberts novel.

The following day was slow and Abigail was grateful for the calm and quiet. She spent the day doing book work, ordering supplies, and reading a new book on cooking gluten-free. At the end of the day, she was starting to close the store when Sheriff Johnson strolled through the door, lifting his hat as he always did when he entered a building.

"I'll be damned, Abigail, I don't know what you saw, or how you saw it, but we found a young man dead in a dumpster behind the Pelican Pub in Tillamook this morning." He nodded to the south side of town. "Anything else you want to tell me?"

Abigail wrung her hands as if they were wet dishrags. It wasn't a dream, as she had hoped. "Ethan, I've done told you everything I know." She looked up at the tall sheriff with fearful eyes.

"It's okay, Abby. I know you're not involved, but while I don't understand it, you definitely have an insight that could be helpful."

Abigail resisted looking at the bottom shelf of the cupboard behind the counter. "I don't understand it either, Ethan."

"There are a few puzzling facts. You saw this happen yesterday morning, but the man was in the bar with his friend last night, and was killed around 2:30 this morning. So you saw this vision before it happened."

Abigail shook her head with disbelief.

"Abigail, this poor guy in the dumpster was stabbed, sliced open with something I've never seen before, well, anyway, it was bad. I need to know what we're dealing with here."

"You mean, what swooped down on this young man and gouged its monstrous claws in and tore him apart?"

Ethan Johnson tilted his head at her. "How could you know that, Abigail? What aren't you telling me?"

"Only the stuff you wouldn't believe. Trust me."

"After the past two days, I'm ready to believe just about anything. I need to know who killed this young man. I need any leads you can give me, no matter how strange they may be."

"So you'd believe me if I told you a dragon has been unleashed upon our quiet community, and is ripping out the hearts of young men?"

Ethan squinted his eyes at her. "I'd prefer a story that sounds a little more plausible."

Abigail straightened up some costume jewelry on the end of the counter. "Wouldn't we all."

"A dragon." Ethan confirmed.

"Yes." Abigail nodded.

They both dropped their gaze to the counter and kept it there until Ethan broke the silence and grabbed his hat. "Well, I need to get back to the station. Thanks Abigail," he said, tipping his hat with a pinch of the brim.

"You're welcome," Abigail replied as she flipped the open sign to closed and latched the door behind him. So much for calm and quiet, she thought as she picked up her bag and made her way to the back of the store and up the stairs.

Abigail slept restless that night, for in her dreams she flew up and down the coast and over the country side. She was soaring above Garibaldi when she caught his scent.

Bo smoked a cigarette as he walked along the sidewalk. At the end of the road, he climbed up the hill and walked into the trees.

Abigail landed and followed. A quarter mile up the path, a twig snapped under her step.

Bo turned. His eyes bulged with terror as he faced the dragon. He dropped the cigarette and ran through the trees.

Abigail could smell his fear. It was intoxicating. She delighted in chasing him, cornering him, and closing in for the kill when he fell and screamed. The long claws ripped his chest. Blood splattered on leaves and rocks. Where is it? Her ears echoed with the pounding of a heart. A different heart. Her head jerked in the direction of the beat.

Abigail's attention was drawn to Main Street. Past the maritime museum, past the coffee shop, to the two-story building facing the marina – Pirate's Plunder antique shop.

She leapt into the sky and glided on the night breeze blowing across the bay. The closer she got to the antique shop, the stronger the heart beat pounded.

Abigail bolted upright in bed and wiped sweat from her forehead. "It's coming after me," she said aloud, "what am I going to do?" She scrambled out of bed and turned on the lamp next to her rocking chair. She frantically threw on the clothes she had set out for the morning, grabbed her jacket and ran down stairs.

The glow of street lights through the store windows guided her to the cupboard where the red velvet box was stashed. She pulled it out and opened it to make sure the cup was safe inside.

Abigail grabbed the flashlight she kept under the counter and headed out the back door.

The dragon was coming for her, she could feel him. She jogged down the road to the edge of the jetty and climbed out on the rocks.

It was low tide. The moon was bright.

Abigail tucked the box into her left arm and scrambled as far out on the rocks as she could. She clutched the box in her hands and lifted her gaze. The dragon loomed before her, staring at her, his gold scales glimmering in the moonlight.

"What do you want from me?" she asked.

The dragon's mouth didn't move, but his voice echoed in her ears, just as she had seen his vision through her eyes. "I want to live." He said. His eyes glimmered.

Abigail's voice shook with fear. "You look alive to me."

The large beast circled around her moving swiftly.

"Looks can be deceiving. I am only partially complete."

She shook a little, her hands trembling. "You need a heart?"

His large head nodded.

"Hopefully not mine?" she asked, terrified to consider the answer. The velvet box in her hands began moving and pulsing, and changing shape.

"No, mine," the dragon snarled. "You hold it in your hands."

Abigail's hands shook so violently she almost dropped the box on the jagged rocks.

The dragon moved closer to her, his eyes on the heart. "Don't drop it! If you drop it we both die!"

"We?" she cried. "Why me?"

"Because we are connected. If you place the heart in my chest, I will grant you any wish." the dragon said as he shoved his chest toward her. The scales slowly spread revealing an opening in the skin. "Go ahead, put it in."

Abigail trembled. Tears poured down her cheeks. Her knees wobbled. She turned away and flinched as she leaned forward and pushed the heart into the gaping hole, hoping she would not be pulled in with it.

Abigail felt the heart lodge into place and quickly stepped backwards nearly stumbling over a rock.

The dragon shuddered; he turned his head to look up to the sky, then back at Abigail. The glare of the moonlight reflecting on his brilliant gold scales stung her eyes.

"Your wish?" he asked.

"Take your vision with you when you go. I don't want to see death anymore. I don't even want to remember that I saw any of this." Abigail replied. She stood straight and threw her shoulders back.

The dragon bowed his head at her, turned, and flew off into the night sky.

Three days later Sheriff Johnson stopped by the Pirate's Plunder antique shop. Abigail was sitting behind the counter as she always did, reading a worn Ann McCaffrey novel, and drinking her tea.

"Mornin', Abigail, I wanted to follow up with you on the young man in the dumpster. We found his buddy in the woods yesterday, killed the same way."

Abigail looked at Ethan Johnson as if he were speaking Japanese. "What on earth are you talking about, Ethan? A man was killed in a dumpster? It sounds terrible. But why would you follow up with me?"

Ethan scratched his chin. "The man who sold you the china, the two guys in your visions."

Abigail bent down the corner of a page and placed the book in her lap. "I haven't bought any china in months, maybe even longer."

"C'mon now, Abby. You're the one that called me in here and told me about it."

"Ethan, the last thing I called you about was that raccoon that broke into my cellar last October. Visions." She laughed. "If I had that power, I wouldn't be a divorcee!"

She shook her head and went back to reading her book. "Men!"

A glint of gold flashed across her eyes.

The power of choice is yours.

BROKEN SKY

The Miracle makes use of time, but is not limited by it.

Carter Webb paced the concrete floor of the large barn to the steady cadence of rain pounding on the metal roof. He stopped to stare at the formula scribbled on the large white board hanging on the west wall, a design for a new sculpture commissioned for the courtyard of the University's math building. He tilted his head and looked at it from a different angle and realized he had written a formula for something far more interesting. His scruffy German wirehaired pointer, Niels, lay next to a large work bench and Carter's cold turkey and swiss sandwich, waiting patiently for scraps that would fall from the plate.

"I think we have something here." Carter said as he took his sandwich, dropped the corner of it for Niels, and took a large bite himself.

Niels barked once in the direction of the door. Carter looked down at him. "Why would someone come over on a night like this?"

The large door swung open and Zoey Jacobs stepped in, shaking the rain out of her frizzy red hair, as she closed the door behind her.

"Zoey, what on earth are you doing out in this rain? And without an umbrella?" Carter asked, as he approached her.

Wrapping her arms around herself, Zoey shuddered as water dripped from the tips of her hair down her back. Carter grabbed an old blanket off a pile used for covers, and wrapped it around her shoulders.

"I was just on my way home from work and my car broke down again about a mile up the road. I need a ride home."

"Sure, but I told you to get that looked at. And where's your rain coat and umbrella?"

"Probably in my coat closet. I'm still getting used to this rain."

"Okay, give me a minute and I'll run you home."

Zoey walked over to the whiteboard and examined the complex formula. "I thought you were a sculptor, not a physicist."

$$\nabla_a(X^b + Y^b) = \nabla_a X^b + \nabla_a Y^b$$
$$\nabla_a(X^b Y^c) = Y^c(\nabla_a X^b) + X^b(\nabla_a Y^c)$$
$$\nabla_a(f(x)X^b) = f\nabla_a X^b + X^b\nabla_a f = f\nabla_a X^b + X^b\frac{\partial f}{\partial x^a}$$
$$\nabla_a(cX^b) = c\nabla_a X^b, \quad c \text{ is constant}$$
$$\nabla_{\vec{A}}\vec{B}(X) = \lim_{\epsilon \to 0}\frac{1}{\epsilon}\left[\Pi_{(\epsilon,0,\gamma)}\vec{B}(\gamma[\epsilon]) - \vec{B}(X)\right]$$
$$G_{ab} + \Lambda g_{ab} = \frac{8\pi G}{c^4}T_{ab}$$

Carter hobbled over on his one good leg and one prosthetic leg to the whiteboard.

"Anyone knows math is the basics of all art, especially sculpture." Carter pointed to the first line of the formula. "I started out with an idea for the university piece, but then I started thinking about Einstein's theory of relativity, so I played with that for a while, and voila!"

Zoey smiled. "Voila, what?"

"Time travel, of course." He laughed.

"What?"

Carter followed the equation with his fingers. "You see, it's all about the maths. When Everette derived the existence of the positron, after taking the square root, we would normally disregard the negative answer because it has no meaning. But he intuited that there was no reason that out rightly suggests a legitimate reason for disregarding that negative value. And some decades later, it was shown in a laboratory that his intuition was correct. Quantum and QFT together represent a deep study of the inter-connectedness in the subtleties in the mechanics of nature." In his own way, Carter was trying to impress Zoey.

"So you're saying time travel is possible, but with math instead of a machine? But how?" Zoey's green eyes sparkled at the mysterious symbols and formulas on the white board.

"Well, it's kind of hard to explain. It has to do with timing and atmospheric pressure."

Zoey's disappointment in the over simplification was lost on Carter, in his excitement of sharing his passion.

"Think of the possibilities. If we could go back and meet people like Plato, or Einstein." His eyes drifted back to the board. "Think about the changes we could effect, knowing what we know now, and having this knowledge back then."

Niels gulped down the last of the turkey and swiss sandwich as Zoey swallowed her astonishment.

"Where would you go?" she asked Carter as he handed her an umbrella and slid his rain coat over her shoulders.

"What do you mean?" Carter asked pulling on another rain coat himself.

"I mean, if you could time travel, where would you go?"

"It's not a matter of where, but when. I can't change the space, only the time."

Carter limped out of the door with Zoey behind him. Niels had pulled the plate off of the bench and was licking it clean.

Carter rubbed his left leg as he started his small pickup.

Zoey fastened her seat belt and looked over at him. "It's still hurting, isn't it?"

He put the pickup in gear and backed out of his carport. "No more than usual."

"What if you could go back, to just before…" She looked down at his leg. "Well, do you think your life would be any different now?"

"Of course." Carter replied as he drove through the heavy rain. "Quantum physics shows that even if I make identical choices, identical events don't necessarily take place."

Zoey waited for Carter to continue, but only silence followed. The lulling sound of the wipers and motor filled the empty space for the next mile.

"Why not?" Zoey asked as Carter pulled into her driveway.

Carter's thoughts were interrupted by a crack of lightening and grumblings of thunder right above their heads. His eyes lit up. "Of course!"

"Of course, what?" Zoey asked.

"Lightning. It's the key element of the equation." Carter said as he put the car in park. "Let me know if you need a ride to your car later, and make sure you carry your umbrella next time." He smiled at her, but his mind was on the equation on the whiteboard.

Zoey pulled the rain coat off from around her shoulders and laid it on the seat. "Thanks again Carter. You're a sweetheart." She leaned across the seat, kissed him on the cheek, jumped out the door and ran to the house.

By the time Carter thought to kiss her back, she was already in the house. He liked Zoey, but there was no time to pursue such frivolity now. He had work to do.

Back in his barn, Carter sat on his chair, rubbing the bulb of the knee that capped the end of his left leg, and stared at the whiteboard. Niels snored in front of the small wood stove in the corner. Zoey's words kept ringing in his brain, what if he could go back and prevent this?

The next lightning storm hit three days later, and Carter wasted no time. He worked meticulously collecting tools and checking weather patterns, so as not to make even the slightest error. He gathered up his notes and looked at his watch. "It's getting late; we have to get out there before the storm is over." He pulled on a poncho, fastened Niels' leash to his collar, grabbed his backpack and headed out the door.

Carter's limp included a bounce as he made his way to his little Toyota pickup. He slid his backpack onto the seat, and Niels jumped in after it.

Carter pulled an old compass out of the pack, set it on the dash, and headed north east. He drove until he reached an old logging road. Driving as slowly as the darkness, rain, and washboard road demanded, the little pickup bounced from rut to rut. Lighting crackled across the black sky and Carter screeched to a halt. He looked at the compass, then poked his head out the window to look up. A split in the clouds gave the impression the sky was broken.

He sat in the pickup with the door open, using the dome light to navigate by parallax using his old compass and his fingers at arm's length to estimate angles. He pulled his notebook out and thumbed through some notes he had written. He grabbed his pack. "This is the place, Niels. We're gonna' make history tonight - experimentally!"

Carter agonized as he pulled himself out of the truck, and placed the compass and other instruments on a rock in a precise configuration. He held an electrometer in his hands and stood on the point indicated on the diagram he made on the ground around him with metal rods from his pack. Niels jumped out of the pickup and started barking.

Carter took his time to carefully arrange his intricately designed instrumentation. When he felt he was fully prepared, and made appropriate notes, he shielded his face from the rain, and held the rods straight up above his head. CRASH! Came the lightning bolt, and Carter disappeared. Niels yelped and whined, but he could not find his master.

For a second or two Carter floated in black, silent emptiness, then a burst of light erupted, and with it, noise and smells he did not recognize. He felt off balance. The rain was gone. Carter stood near the road, but it was day and the sky was blue. Burley men in thick beards trudged past him yelling to each other. One man slapped the hind quarter of a horse strapped to a large freshly cut tree.

Carter was in the middle of a logging camp, but there were no cranes, or screams of chainsaws, just brawny lumberjacks covered in grime, with large axes and tree saws. He stood rigid, taking it all in.

I did it, Carter thought. I'm in the same place, but definitely a different time. This equipment is 70 or 80 years old. He chuckled at the implications of his success.

"Get outta' the way boy, 'less you wanna' ride with the bark. Tree's comin' down!"

Carter ran over to the side of the clearing and noticed it didn't hurt. He smiled as he bent over and ran his hands up his left leg. No prosthetic, it was all his!

"What you grinnin' for?" The burly man with a face covered in black hair snarled. "No one called a break yet, get back to work!"

Carter shoved the rods in his pocket and looked around for Niels, but the dog was not with him. "Sorry," he said to the crew leader, "my first day, what should I do?"

115

The large man shouted back, "Help clear this mess outa' the way. Keep these trees comin' down. Too hot to stand around."

Carter wiped his brow. It had to be at least a hundred degrees, hotter than he'd ever known it to be in these woods. The familiar humidity was almost non-existent. He pulled some slash out of the way, and called over to the man next to him. "What time is it?"

"Nearly lunch time, I 'spect by the smell of it." He answered.

Carter had a sick feeling in his gut. "What operation is this?"

The man looked at him strange, then spit some tobacco to his side and grabbed a log. "Boy, you're workin' for the best company in these parts. Andrew Hammond's bunch. Right now we're on the slopes above the North Fork of Gales Creek. You know, west of Forest Grove. Where'd you think you was?" The man laughed.

Carter kept working. "No, I knew that. I mean, what's the date today?"

The man stopped and looked at Carter is if he were an alien. "Boy, where you from? It's August 14th, 1933. Now I want to eat some lunch soon, so if you don't mind getting' back to work!" He turned and spit some more tobacco out.

Carter stood stunned. "August 14th, 1933? Just about noon?" His face was filled with panic, his heart raced.

"What's wrong with you boy? You sick or somethin'?"

He whimpered. "It starts today. The Tillamook Burn. Right here, right now."

The man shrugged and went back to work.

A few yards away some loggers dragged a Douglas-fir log across a downed tree. The snag erupted into flames that threw sparks in every direction. Within the hour the fire burned through sixty acres. Carter and the loggers fought as best they could with their shovels and hoes, throwing dirt on flames, but it was useless. The fire was better equipped than they were.

Carter had never worked as hard as he did for the next three days. The loggers fought the fire in shifts, but it only grew larger. Fire crews came in from the north and the south to fight the giant blaze. They pulled water wagons, dug containment ditches, and gave it every effort their aching bones could give. But it was no use.

On the fourth day while Carter cleared slash, he heard someone yelling at him. He turned just in time to see a horse rear up and an exploding Douglas fir crash down toward him. He fell backwards and the tree fell across his legs. He screamed in pain. Three men ran to his side. One started shoveling dirt onto the flames. With the strength of Goliath, two men pulled the tree up enough that a third man was able to pull Carter out from under it.

The lumberjacks carried Carter to a tented area and laid him on the ground. Doc Townsend, a tall, skinny man with wiry hair and round glasses, inspected Carter's legs. "Don't worry son, we'll get you taken care of. You're one of the lucky ones."

He winked at Carter and handed him a bottle of whiskey, then proceeded to clean the burned legs.

The whiskey helped, but not much. The pain was excrutiating. Carter tried to rise up to look.

"No, no. You stay down. This is goin' to take some work here. It smashed you up pretty bad. They're both busted, but I think I can save the right one."

Carter took a big swig of whiskey, laid back, turned his head to the side, and cried.

Two days later he woke in a daze. The medical tent was twice as full as the day he was brought in there. The smell of burnt flesh filled his nostrils and turned his stomach.

A young nurse with red wavy hair pulled back under a white cap, rushed to his side. "Are you alright sir? Can I get you some water?"

"Have I met you before?" Carter asked.

She smiled warmly. "Why sir, I been feeding you and wiping your fever away since they brought you in. I'm Ginny, remember?"

He closed his eyes and rolled his head back and forth. "I don't hardly remember anything, Miss Ginny. Only that my legs hurt."

"They've taken the left leg, but the right is looking much better today."

"My leg? How will I work with only one leg?" A tear rolled down the side of his face.

"Doc Townsend has some crutches for you when you're ready. I can help you with them, if you'd like."

Carter smiled and placed his hand on hers. "I would like that. My head is in such a fog."

"Don't fret, you'll be better in time." She dipped a rag in a bucket of cool water, rung it out, and tenderly spread it across his forehead.

Carter panned the view from his cot. "I know my memory is spotty, but I don't feel like I should be here."

Ginny smiled at him. "I'm sure the shock of your accident has turned your mind upside down, but you're in good hands."

Two weeks later, Carter walked out of the make shift hospital on his right leg and a pair of crutches. Ginny helped him onto a pack mule and handed his crutch up to him.

"I'm staying at the Garibaldi boarding house. Will you come to see me there?" Carter asked with hopeful eyes.

Ginny smiled. "Of course I will."

The mule took Carter through the trees and brush to the road at the bottom where a car waited to take him into town.

Carter sat on the porch of the boarding house and watched the birds fly over the bay. It started to rain. He inhaled deep and smiled, enjoying the fresh smell of rain-washed air. "Nicholas, come help me." He called out to the son of Mrs. Downs, the boarding house owner.

Nicholas was a stout young man of twelve years, with curly hair and a face full of freckles. "Yes sir, what do you need help with?"

Carter leaned forward and grabbed his crutches. "Help me get up to my room, lad. I'm tired and need to turn in."

"Momma switched your room sir, seein's how you have such a hard time with the stairs. She put your things in the room off the back porch. Be easier for you there, just go through the kitchen."

Carter winked at the boy. "Well you're just full of all kinds of help today. Come on, give me a hand up."

Nicholas walked through the house with Carter, past the large kitchen, and left into a small room with a twin bed and a small table. "Momma put fresh water in your bowl and a clean towel for you."

Carter walked over to the table with the wash bowl, and observed the stubble on his face in the mirror above it. He noticed a bag on the side of the wash bowl and emptied it out. He looked at the rods, and equipment in a strange way. "What manner of things are these?"

"I don't know sir. Momma said they was yours. You brought them with you."

Carter picked up the electrometer and turned it around, examining it from different angles. "I think you're right lad, I think this is mine. Leave me be now, I'll be fine."

The boy excused himself and shut the door behind him.

Carter sorted through the strange tools. "I know these things. Why can't I remember them? It's like a dream that sits on the edge of my mind." He limped over to the bed and sat down with the compass in his hands. "Where did you come from?" He asked it, before easing back on the bed and fell into a restless sleep.

The morning's sun and crowing roosters woke Carter. He could hear Nicholas and Mrs. Downs feeding the chickens in the yard. What am I going to do? He wondered as he pulled the quilt back and looked at the stub of his leg. What work can a man do if he cannot perform labor?

"Mr. Carter, are you awake?" Ginny asked from the other side of his door.

His heart leapt. "Yes ma'am I am. But I'm afraid I'm not decent for company."

"But sir, I've seen you in worse, I'm sure. I've come by to join you for breakfast."

"I'll be there in just a few minutes."

Carter splashed some cool water from the basin on his face and wiped it off. He brushed his hair and hobbled out on his crutches to the large table in the dining room.

Ginny sat next to an empty chair at the table. She smiled up at him. "I've saved you a spot. Do you need some help?" She started to get up, but he shook his head.

"No, you stay seated. I can make my own way just fine."

"I thought if you felt up to it, we might go for a picnic this evening. I could make a basket and come by in my father's car?"

Carter loved the way she looked at him, it almost made him forget the pain in his leg. "I'd like that Miss Ginny."

They ate their breakfast in quiet, occasionally looking at each other.

Carter spent the day sitting in a rocking chair on the front porch, drinking lemonade and waiting for the day to be done.

All he could think about now was the lovely young Miss Ginny, how her wavy red hair fell down in her face, and her green eyes sparkled when she looked at him.

Nicholas joined him in the late afternoon.

"You done with your chores, Nicholas?"

"Yes sir. Momma said I could take me a break. Thought I'd sit out here with you."

"Your momma's a good woman. She runs a fine boardin' house here."

Nicholas nodded, sat on the steps, and wrapped his arms around his knees as he pulled them close to his chest. "You like Miss Ginny, sir?"

Carter smiled. "And what business would that be of yours, Mr. Downs?" They both laughed.

Ginny pulled up in a jalopy. "Are you ready for the finest fried chicken and biscuits in town?" She grinned up at Carter.

"Yes ma'am, I am." Carter struggled at getting up out of the rocker. It was taking him longer than he'd hoped to get adjusted to having only one leg. But he was determined to be strong, especially for Ginny.

As they started to pull away from the house, Nicholas came running back out with the small black draw string bag in his hands. He held it up to Carter. "You don't want to forget your things, sir. You may need them."

Carter was hesitant to take the bag, not sure what the boy meant. But he stuffed it in his inside jacket pocket.

Getting out of the vehicle with only one leg proved more complicated than Carter had anticipated. He fell to the ground, but Ginny was there to help him. They sat for a moment with him across her lap, laughing at each other.

"Come on now, you can help me set things up."

Carter got to his feet and followed Ginny to the blanket she had spread on the ground under a large tree. From this spot they could see the ocean. The evening air was cool. The ground was mostly scorched from the Tillamook burn, the largest forest fire in history. He didn't know how she had managed to find a green spot on the hillside, but he was glad she did.

Ginny filled Carter's plate with her attempts to win his heart. The fried chicken was better than she claimed, and he devoured a double helping. With his belly full, he laid down beside her and looked up at the clear sky. His face twitched as if a fly was buzzing past his nose.

"What is it Carter, are you alright?"

Carter wiped his brow. "I keep getting flashes of light, and glimpses of something, but it goes so fast I can't quite make it out."

"Ever since the accident?" Ginny asked.

"Yes, I think I'm going to remember something, and then it's gone."

Suddenly the wind changed and blew a storm in from the north. Dark clouds poured across the sky, by the time they had the picnic packed into the trunk, the couple was drenched from rain. They laughed again as they scrambled into the car to wait out the storm. Ginny leaned over and kissed Carter on the cheek.

"Zoey!"

Ginny pushed back. "Who is that?"

"You. You're Zoey."

She looked at him confused and devastated. "I'm Ginny."

Carter struggled more with his thoughts now than his leg. What was happening to him? He felt for the pouch in his jacket pocket, and pulled it out. He looked at the compass and suddenly remembered. "Ginny, help me."

"In this rain?"

Carter nodded yes.

Ginny helped him out of the car and lay the items on the ground.

"I know this seems crazy Ginny, but I have to try this." He yelled through the lightning and the pouring rain. "Go wait for me in the car, I'll be fine."

Ginny climbed back in the car to wait and watch.

Carter's memory was fading in and out like a blinking light. He had to hurry while he could still remember. Everything was in place, he looked up and stretched his arms and the rods t the sky.

Crash! Blackness. The feeling of being tossed around in a small boat at sea. New sounds, new smells, new surroundings. Carter sat up and pushed his hair back from his face. He leaned forward and witnessed once again, he had no amputation, stump or prosthetic, but two fully functional legs. I must be more careful this time, he thought, I must keep my legs.

Carter couldn't shake thoughts of how much Ginny looked like Zoey. He must note that. It was amazing too, he wrote, that his mind had adjusted to the surrounding time. But he remembered who he was now, and he remembered his science. He was relieved.

Carter stood up, surveyed his surroundings, looking in all directions to get his bearings and assess the situation. It was cluttered, noisy and unwelcoming, but it didn't appear to be dangerous. There were a few trees behind him surrounded by a fence. Everything else was paved. Now it was a forest of buildings piled one on top of the other. It reminded him of Hong Kong.

Carter walked through streets and mused at the transformations, logging the surroundings in to the database of his mind. There were no cars, only a rail system. A sleek passenger train swooshed by him. He continued down the hill to the lookout point. Tillamook Bay was gone, and in its place stood a giant metal structure blocking the view of the ocean. He hiked into a town that should have been Garibaldi. Glass and metal buildings rose up to block the sun. The marina, the boats, and the docks were replaced by structures that blinded him as they reflected the sunlight. Surely we still fish? He thought.

A neon sign flashed rotating messages at the edge of town. Welcome to Garibaldi. Carter let out a sigh of relief. But how did our small fishing village become this? He asked himself, as he picked up his step, smiling once again at having both of his legs and feet. The air smelled like oil and grease, accompanied by sounds of mechanical engines churning, and metal clanking. The wafting of fish on the ocean breeze was only a memory here.

Tall buildings connected and overhung at the center of town, obscuring the sky. Trees and vegetation were taken over by concrete and metal frameworks. Plants were confined to glassed-in greenhouses. It was like the science fiction movies he watched a as kid. What about meat? He wondered. He walked on.

The center of the small town was crowded with merchants and shoppers, people moving, no one standing still. It made him dizzy. He heard a dog bark, but didn't see any animals. The sun didn't reach the street, leaving this world to be lit by neon. He walked to where his home had been. But it was gone, replaced by endless structures that reached to the sky. Rain fell and drizzled down the sides of the buildings, but not in the center, as if a shield spread between them.

People pushed and shoved past Carter. They weren't dressed so different. Just as many zippers and clips, but in more bizarre cuts and shapes. Their hair was every color of the rainbow, and women had lipstick that seemed to change color with every movement of their mouths. Everyone had on sunglasses. He couldn't see any eyes. Maybe that's why they didn't see him?

A piece of machinery zipped past his leg so close he could feel the blade. It startled him. He jumped out of the way and backed up against a concrete wall to catch his breath. He looked at a food vendor next to him. "Don't want to lose a leg." He chuckled, trying to make small talk. But the vendor didn't acknowledge him.

Carter walked into a convenience store. It was hard to move anywhere, inside or out, the people were so thick. He looked at a clerk behind the counter. "What day is it? Do you have a newspaper?"

She didn't look at him either, but pointed to a monitor above her head displaying a futuristic version of CNN. News captions streamed across the screen, and then the date – November 12, 2431. Carter smiled. He walked over to an older man sitting in a corner watching a small screen in his hand. It looked like a piece of clear plastic, but the screen was streaming video.

"I almost lost my leg out there, some crazy little thing zipped by me so fast."

The older man didn't look up, but tapped his leg. Carter knew the sound well from his work on metal. "They replace them fast enough. No need to worry about that." He said.

Carter gulped. Nausea rolled around his stomach. What had become of everyone? They didn't even seem human anymore. Where were the dogs? Where was nature? Panic grasped him. He went back outside and stood against the building, watching people. The color of their hair changed as they moved, even their facial features seemed to transform as they talked. Who were these people? What was life to them?

Carter stumbled to a narrow, dirty alley way, and fell on a pile of trash. He could hardly breathe. "I have to get home before I become one of them." He pushed his way back through the crowds and up the hill toward the small patch of trees.

There is nothing in time for a traveler, Carter realized, as waited for the rain, the wind, and the lightning that would take him back home.

You think if you could travel in time you could change the world. Instead, the world changes you.

SHADOWS KEEP

The abilities you possess are only shadows of your real strength.

Broken and fallen branches obstructed the way into the Tillamook State Forest. The dirt road was rutted and slippery from the recent rain. Aiden's '65 Toyota Land Cruiser conquered every obstacle nature threw in his path. He stopped and looked down at the hand drawn map on the seat beside him. He was lost. This wasn't the road Charlie described.

Little light found its way through the drizzle and thick trees in the late afternoon. In the distance, a pillar of smoke called to him.

Aiden shifted the Land Cruiser into first gear and slowly crawled over the rocks and fallen branches of the so-called forest service road. Just over a ridge sat a cherry red '67 Ford Fairlane with the hood up and steam pouring out of the radiator. A damsel in distress, and he was here to save her. She stood next to the car, obviously waiting for help. He stopped the Land Cruiser and jumped out. He smiled at her loose tee-shirt and tight cutoff jeans, and the beautiful sea of golden waves that fell down her back.

Getting lost might not be bad after all, Aiden thought.

She pointed to the engine. "I don't know what happened, but it's not running."

"Did you call for help?"

"I called you." She smiled.

"Good thing I can read smoke signals." Aiden laughed. He stepped up, looked at the steam pouring out of the radiator. "Looks like it's overheated. After it cools down we can add some water and you'll be back on the road in no time." He held out his hand to her. "I'm Aiden."

She shook his hand and flashed a seductive smile. "Andrea. I haven't seen you around here before."

Aiden smiled, trying to hide his braces. "I'm from Colorado, that's where I'm going to college. But I'm here for the summer working at my uncle's coffee shop."

Andrea took a few steps and looked back at him. "So what are you doing up here?"

"I'm meeting my friend. We're supposed to go fishing this weekend."

"Maybe he already made it to town?"

Aiden looked around, not seeing anything but trees. "What town?"

Andrea giggled, "Shadows Keep, of course. The only town this side of the Tillamook burn." She ran her fingers sensuously along the lines of the car. "Where is your uncle's place?"

Aiden walked around the car and ran his tongue across his braces. "Garibaldi. I haven't ever seen you there."

"Actually, I've never been out of Shadows Keep. But my boyfriend and I are planning on going to Portland soon. I can't wait to see a big city."

"So where is Shadows Keep?"

Andrea pointed between some trees to the right. "It's just up there a ways. You're not far from it."

Aiden tried to touch the radiator cap, but it was still too hot. "Let me get a rag and get this cap off. I have some water in my rig. We should be able to pour it in soon." He walked to his Land Cruiser and pulled out a gallon jug of water and an old rag from a tool box. He headed back to the car, but Andrea was gone.

"Andrea! Andrea!" His words echoed through the forest. All he heard was an animal in the distance and the wind rustling through the heavy tree branches. He placed the rag on the radiator cap.

"What the?" Aiden dropped the rag and felt the engine. Every part of the car was ghostly cold.

Aiden walked slowly backwards to his Land Cruiser and put his things away. He turned the key in the ignition. Nothing. Not even a groan. Aiden pulled out his cell phone. Of course, he thought, no service here. He stuck it in his pocket, pulled up the hood of his vehicle, everything looked fine. He fiddled with it for nearly twenty minutes. It was simply dead, as dead as the Fairlane in front of him.

It was getting late, dark, and cold. Aiden slid his keys in his pocket and grabbed his backpack. He pulled a flashlight out of the glove box and headed up through the trees toward Shadows Keep.

The sun disappeared as fast as Andrea did. Strange sounds emanated from tree tops and underbrush. Aiden trembled a little from the cold in the air and the fear in his mind. It was not a good combination. His feet ached by the time he reached a small clearing in the middle of the woods. The clouds separated just enough to let a ray of moonlight reflect on the windows of the few buildings that made up the small community of Shadows Keep. No population sign, Aiden noticed. What's the point when it's less than ten? He gulped his anxiety down and headed for the one building that seemed to have life inside.

The Shadows Keep store, post office, restaurant and bar were all housed in one two-story building with a large screened-in porch the entire length of it. Aiden walked in and nodded at the lady behind the store counter. He looked into the next room which was the bar and restaurant. "Still open?" He asked.

The clerk grinned wide, her mouth exposing more gaps than teeth. "Visitors are always welcome. We don't close till the sun comes up, or everyone goes home. Whichever happens first." She laughed with a low belly laugh that made Aiden uncomfortable. He watched her close as he headed for the doorway. "They aren't vampires or werewolves, are they?" He joked.

The clerk laughed harder at him. "Maybe you want to buy some garlic before you step in?"

Aiden realized how ridiculous he sounded, and joined her in a laugh of his own. But he watched his step, nonetheless. As he entered the small room with four tables, a bar and two rocking chairs in front of a wood stove, Aiden looked in the windows to make sure the four people in there all had a reflection. They did. He was safe for now.

Aiden sat on a stool at the bar. An Asian lady with a large tattoo of bright orange and red flames that ran from her neck to her left wrist, placed a coaster in front of him. "What'll you have?"

"Beer," Aiden looked at the tap handles, "Fat Tire would be great."

She grabbed a frosted glass and filled it with the amber liquid that Aiden hoped would help calm his nerves. He drained the glass in a series of continuous gulps before setting it down. He swiveled around to look at the two older men in the rocking chairs. They peered over their shoulders to look back at Aiden.

The man sitting in the rocking chair on the right stood up, he was nearly seven feet tall, and wore a ball cap that looked like it had been pulled out of a fire. In fact, Aiden noticed, everyone in the room looked, and smelled, like they'd just come off a fire line. Smoke jumpers? He wondered.

The man walked over to the bar, twirled the toothpick in his mouth with great precision. He never took his eyes off of Aiden. "Another, Wendy." He said as he pushed his empty glass to the lady behind the counter. Wendy poured it full of beer and pushed it back.

Aiden felt the sweat beading on the top layer of his skin under the scrutinizing look of this monster man. As long as he didn't open his mouth to expose two large fangs, Aiden would be okay.

The tall man took a drink, squinted one eye at Aiden. "I'm the sheriff here, Sheriff Partin. What's your business in Shadows Keep?"

Aiden wrenched his neck a little trying to regain a normal breath. "Um, just, well…" He knew the words were in there somewhere, he was having a hard time finding them though.

"Well, spit it out boy." Sheriff Partin said impatiently.

"I…my Land Cruiser died down the road a ways back. I stopped to help a girl with her car, and then mine wouldn't start. She told me the town was right up here so I headed this way. Thought she might be here."

A slender man with buck teeth sat at a table playing solitaire. He looked up at Aiden. "What girl?"

Aiden wiped the sweat back from his brow and finished his drink. "I can't remember her name. Cute. She said she was from here."

Sheriff Partin leaned in close and spoke in a low voice. "Everyone that is from here, *is* here. You must be mistaken."

Aiden looked confused. "Sure, okay. Well, I was supposed to meet my buddy, Charlie. Charlie Enders? Anyway, he's got a fishing trip planned for us. I guess I took a wrong turn somewhere."

The man playing solitaire looked over at him again. "No Charlie Enders here." He laid a red six down on a black seven.

"I was supposed to meet him at some camp on the Nehalem River. He said it's the best fishing. Do you know how to get there from here?"

The man at the table put down his cards. "You've got quite a ways to go boy. And it's late."

Sheriff Partin sat his empty glass down again. "These woods ain't safe at night."

"Maybe you better stay here tonight, start out in the morning." Said the man at the table, as he aimed an uncomfortable smile at Aiden.

Aiden looked at his watch, it was half past nine. Time seemed to disappear with everything else. "Don't suppose there's a hotel room in town anywhere?"

Low snickers filled the room. Aiden was nervous, his stomach hurt, and his chest felt constricted with every breath. "Don't suppose there's a mechanic in town either?"

The man at the table pulled the bill of his ball cap around to the back of his head. He was dressed in overalls and muddy leather boots. "I'm the town mechanic. Name's Bob. No hotel, but I do have a fairly decent couch you can bunk on for the night if you want?"

Aiden's muscles tensed up. As long as there were no dueling banjos, he might live through the night. He turned to Wendy behind the bar. "Can I have another beer?"

Bob's black lab lay on the floor next to him. She didn't move until Bob put the cards in the box and stood up. The dog slowly stretched and stood beside him. He looked over at Aiden. "You comin'?"

Aiden downed his beer in one gulp, put a couple of dollars on the counter and slid off the stool. He took a deep breath and followed Bob out. Sheriff Partin watched him closely out of the corner of his eye.

There were no sidewalks or paved streets in Shadows Keep. Just gravel and mud. Lots of mud. Bob walked past a gas pump and a small garage. A few yards past that sat a newer building. Bob pointed to it as they passed by. "That's the fire station and police station. I live right behind it." Around the building and across a gravel roadway sat a small log house with several deer antlers hanging on the outside wall of the porch.

"Do you think you can take me back to my Land Cruiser tomorrow, take a look at it?" Aiden asked.

Bob nodded. "Sure. I've got a tow truck in the garage. For now, get some sleep."

The house was dim inside with a small floor lamp in one corner. A recliner held together by silver duct tape, sat on one side of a wood stove, and a very old sagging-in-the-middle couch draped by raggedy hand crochet afghans on the other side. Bob handed a blanket and dingy pillow to Aiden, smiled, and disappeared into the bedroom.

Aiden stood looking at the bedding, the couch, and the floor. He wasn't sure which was cleaner, or at this point, less dirty. He opted for the couch. He had a hard time falling asleep with the constant feeling of something multi-legged crawling across him. Exhaustion won out and he fell asleep. He had buried his head in the pillow that smelled like a wet dog, and nearly strangled himself with one of the afghans around his neck. In a gasp for air, Aiden sat bolt up on the couch. The room was pitch black with a hint of moonlight peering through the reproduction of a rebel flag draped across the window. He pulled the afghan away from his neck and threw it on the floor. He sniffed the air and frowned at the smell of charred wood and smoke. He heard footsteps in the gravel outside, a shadow passed the window.

"Who's there?" Aiden said, almost loud enough for someone to hear. It was probably no one. Or maybe just a dog, a coyote, a bear? Best he stay inside, where it was safe. He slumped back down in the sagging couch, his eyes never leaving the window.

There it was again, the sound of footsteps. Aiden sat up quickly and tiptoed to the window. It was the girl with the broken down car. He could see her sitting on a stump next to a wood pile. She was beautiful in the moonlight, almost ethereal. He slipped on his shoes and grabbed his jacket, quietly slipping out the front door.

The rest of the small town was asleep. No one stirred, no lights were on. Aiden walked up to her. "Hey, it's me, Aiden. Remember? I stopped to help you."

Andrea smiled as she recognized him. "Oh yeah, I remember you."

Aiden shoved his hands deep in his pockets. "So you live here?"

Andrea pointed to the two story yellow house across from the white building that doubled as a church and masonic lodge. "I live there with my grandmother." She took a cigarette out and lit it, inhaling slowly, she looked at Aiden and held the pack out to him.

Aiden hunched his shoulders to ward off the night's cold. "No thanks, I don't smoke."

She shrugged and put the pack back in her jacket pocket. Andrea took another drag. "Suit yourself."

"What was your name again? Sorry, I'm really bad with names." Aiden felt embarrassed.

"It's Andrea. You're cute."

Aiden felt the warm blush wash over his face.

"Well, I better get back in. Granny tends to freak out if she checks in on me and I'm not there." She took a final drag from the cigarette and put it out in the dirt. "I'll see you around."

"Yeah." Was all Aiden could think of. He never was good at being suave with the girls. He watched her walk to the yellow house and disappear around the back.

A snap of twigs caught his attention. Aiden didn't want to wait around to see who or what was moving in the dark. He sprinted for the door of Bob's house and latched it behind him.

The morning sun hit Aiden in the eyes and rudely woke him up, followed by the smell of hot coffee from the small kitchen. He got up and followed his nose. Bob nodded to a rack of cups on the wall. "Help yourself."

Aiden didn't waste any time pouring the hot black elixir into his mouth. He sat down in one of the two chairs at the breakfast table. "Can we go get my Land Cruiser this morning? I really gotta' get it fixed and get back to town. I'll have to catch my buddy next time."

Bob finished his coffee and rubbed his crotch. "Sure thing. Let me get my gear and we'll be on our way."

The black lab sat staring at the door. Bob opened the door and she ran out. "Soon as she comes back, we'll leave."

Aiden was restless, his back hurt from the lumpy couch. He really needed to brush his teeth. "I think I'll get some fresh air, see you outside." Aiden finished his coffee, and headed out the back door.

The mountain air smelled fresh and crisp in the morning. A fragrance of pine and spruce delighted his nostrils. The black lab ran and dove into a large pile of leaves and tree limbs behind the fire and police station. She started digging in the pile as if a great treasure were buried deep. Aiden wandered over to watch her. She was a pretty dog, shiny coat, good build for a lab.

The dog shoved her head deep in the pile and pulled out a severed arm in her mouth.

A charred human severed arm.

Aiden looked at it, he felt a little dizzy and fell backwards, flat on his back. He caught his breath and sat up, watched the dog run around and start to dig a hole a few yards away, no doubt to bury the arm.

Aiden was speechless, he pointed to the dog and her treasure, but he couldn't get any words to come out. He jumped up and ran around the building and into the fire and police station.

Sheriff Partin sat at a desk, his feet up on the corner, drinking his morning coffee. He squinted his eyes at Aiden, who came in waving his arms like some extinct bird, making similar sounds. "Speak boy, what is it?"

Aiden leaned forward, put his hands on his knees and tried to catch his breath. He looked up at Sheriff Partin with panic on his face. "Sheriff, arm, severed arm, dog!"

Sheriff Partin stood up slowly, walked around Aiden sizing him up and down. "Just how much did you drink last night, boy?"

Aiden motioned for the Sheriff to follow him. "Come on, see it." He ran out and to the back of the building with Sheriff Partin close behind. The lab was still digging, and the burnt arm lay on the ground next to her.

Sheriff Partin bent over and looked close, then stood back up. "Well I'll be damned. That's an arm." He looked back at Aiden.

Aiden was still panting; he shrugged and pointed to the dog. "See, told you."

Sheriff Partin rubbed the back of his neck. "Now tell me where the rest of the body is."

Aiden squealed like a stuck pig. "What? How the hell should I know? The dog dug that up out of your trash pile." He pointed to the large pile of leaves and tree limbs.

Sheriff Partin walked over to the pile. "Guess we better go through this then. Make use of yourself boy, grab a rake back there and start sifting."

Aiden backed up shaking his head. "Not me. I'm not cut out for this kind of stuff. I gotta' get back to my rig, back to town, where living people are. Shouldn't you wait for more authorities? You know, don't disturb the crime scene, all that kind of stuff?"

"Boy, you watch way too much television. This is my crime scene, I'm the law, and no one else is going to come up here and help us."

Bob walked up behind him. "What you got Sheriff?"

Sheriff Partin pointed to the arm and explained the situation.

Tony came walking down the road, a short older man with a goatee more grey than brown. He waved. "Hey Sheriff, Hey Bob. Mornin' to ya'."

Sheriff Partin called over. "Tony, I need some help."

They raked through the pile while the Sheriff got a plastic bag and sealed the arm in it. The dog dropped her head and whined. Aiden watched him wrap it up and seal it with strapping tape. "What are you going to do? Who is it?"

Sheriff Partin shrugged. "Looks like possibly a girl's arm from the size. Hard to say. We ain't got a forensics lab up here. I'll take it over to the morgue and call down to the valley, see if they can take it, find out something more."

Aiden looked around to the five buildings that made up the town. "Morgue?"

Sheriff Partin nodded to the two-story white building. "Masonic lodge, church, morgue in the basement. You could stick around, help us look for more parts."

"I appreciate the offer Sheriff, really, but I think I better get going."

"Suit yourself." Sheriff Partin said, and headed off to the morgue with the plastic bundle stuck under his arm.

Bob scratched his head and spit on the ground. "Well, we best get your rig towed up here so we can figure out what it needs." Bob headed to the small garage next to the Shadows

Keep general store, bar and restaurant. Aiden quickly followed him. The black lab beat them both to the truck.

Bob opened the passenger door of the old tow truck for the dog to jump in, and Aiden followed her. Bob went around to the other side and climbed in, started it up and headed down the mountain.

Aiden noticed red smears all over the floor boards of the truck, and even some on the seat. He looked around and spied the ax at the side of the seat. "Bob, what's all over the floor here?"

Bob glanced over as the truck bounced down the dirt road through tall trees and short bursts of sunlight. "Oh, blood. Don't worry, it's dry."

"Blood?" Aiden gulped.

"Yep, hit a deer awhile back, didn't want to waste it. Know what I mean?" Bob chuckled. Aiden's stomach churned.

"How far down did you say it was?" Bob asked.

Aiden glanced out the window, but nothing looked familiar. "I thought it was along here somewhere. There was an old Ford Fairlane too. We should see both of them."

Bob stomped on the brakes and the truck fish tailed as it came to a stop. "Are you leadin' me on some empty beer run? I got more to do than be the butt of your practical jokes. And I'm chargin' you for this!"

Aiden's nausea was in full swing. "Bob, seriously, it was right in here, somewhere."

Bob pulled on the steering wheel and turned the truck around, stomped on the gas and headed back up the hill to Shadows Keep.

"Wait! Where are you going? Aren't you going to get my rig?" Aiden yelped.

Bob spit out the window and squinted as he looked over at Aiden. "You ain't got no rig. You walked to town."

Aiden slumped down in his seat and whimpered. The lab laid her chin on his knee, looking up at him with sympathetic eyes.

Bob pulled back into the garage and they all got out. Bob motioned for Aiden to follow as he headed to a junk yard of old cars and parts behind the garage.

"There." Bob pointed to a rusted out '67 Ford Fairlane in the back, dusty and dirty, covered by other car parts. "There's your Ford Fairlane. That's been here for five years." Bob spit to the side, and scratched his head. "Come to think of it, five years ago yesterday."

Aiden turned sufficiently pale as if all the blood had drained out of his body. He stuttered. "Then where's Andrea? The girl that was driving it?"

Bob narrowed his eyes at Aiden. "How'd you know her name?"

"I told you, I stopped to help her when her radiator overheated."

"Like I told you boy, she disappeared…five years ago yesterday. All we ever found was her car, an ax in the back seat and a whole lotta' blood. And you best not be bringing up old wounds like that to the Sheriff about his niece." He spit on the ground again and glared at Aiden.

"Whole lotta' blood, huh?" Aiden stammered.

"Uh huh."

"Think I'll go get a cup of coffee, or maybe a shot of whiskey." Aiden said as he walked backwards out of the yard.

Aiden kept running it over in his mind as he headed into the restaurant; he saw that car on the road, and Andrea. He ordered two eggs over easy, toast and bacon, coffee black and a shot of Jack Daniels. It was time to get serious!

Wendy placed his order in front of him. The bacon and toast were burnt. "You get your car?"

Aiden picked up the shot glass, tossed his head back and swallowed the whiskey. "Nope. No car. Gonna' be walking home." He shuddered all over and ate his breakfast.

Wendy smiled, picked up the empty shot glass. "Another one?"

"Yes please." Aiden said as he bit the crispy bacon.

Wendy smiled. "Don't worry boy, things aren't always what they seem in Shadows Keep." She headed back to the bar, poured another shot of Jack Daniels, and put it next to his plate.

Aiden pushed his half-eaten breakfast aside and downed the second shot. He sat and stared out the window for a while trying to figure out a way to get back home. Maybe one more shot for the road. The whiskey tasted good.

Aiden thanked Wendy and gave her a generous tip, put his jacket on and started down the road. Wherever it would take him, it had to be better than this crazy place.

Aiden walked for hours, his feet hurt, he was getting hungry, and there was no sign of anything anywhere except trees and more trees. He wasn't sure if he was going in the right direction, but he was going downhill, that had to account for something. His back and head hurt as much as his feet. He wanted to soak in a nice hot bath, or maybe have another shot of that whisky! He kept walking.

Aiden heard a rumble of an engine and ran in circles trying to figure out where the noise was coming from. It got louder as it got closer.

Yes! It was a vehicle! Aiden ran into its path, jumping and waving his hands. The green pickup stopped and a man in a uniform got out.

"What you doin' clear out here?" the man asked.

"My Land Cruiser broke down and I was walking back home." Aiden ran up to the pickup. "Can you give me a ride?" He felt relief surge through all of his aching muscles and joints.

The Fish and Game officer nodded for him to get in the pickup. "Sure thing. It's been a crazy storm up here for days. Where have you been?"

Aiden enjoyed the clean cab, the comfortable seat. "I spent last night in Shadows Keep. I don't know where my Land Cruiser is, we tried to find it, but we couldn't."

The officer drove along the bumpy dirt road; he gave Aiden a skeptical look. "Shadows Keep? You crazy?"

Aiden snorted a short laugh. "No, but the people in that town sure are." He shook his head.

The officer shook his head as well. "Boy, I don't know where you were, but the little town of Shadows Keep burnt clean to the ground in a forest fire five years back. There's not a soul or a building left."

Aiden turned another shade of pale.

"Who were you with?" The officer asked.

"What do you mean?"

"You said 'we', I assume you were with someone?"

Aiden shook his head. "I meant, I looked. Maybe it was the whiskey?"

The officer laughed. "Yep, that'll do it every time."

Aiden watched out the window as they drove out of the forest. Little light made its way through the thick trees.

What if you recognized this world was an hallucination? What if you really understood you made it up?

DREAM CATCHER

In dreams we see the truth.

Sheriff Johnson stood on the edge of the Bayocean jetty. The water slapped against the dark rocks, waves pulled the beach houses down off their foundations, dragging them into the unforgiving ocean. He stepped further out on shifting rocks.

A young woman was trapped in a small red car, a dream catcher dangled from her rearview mirror, her wrists handcuffed to the steering wheel. The car slid off the rocks into the tide, water rapidly engulfing it. Her brown eyes pleaded for help. Ethan dove off the rocks to save her, but the car was beyond his reach. She was lost. Only the dream catcher remained, floating on the crest of a wave.

In a gasp for air, Ethan woke up from the nightmare. He searched for clues to the dream's meaning. Did it relate to something he was working on? He shook his head and got out of bed. Nothing came to mind.

Ethan got dressed for the day in his favorite jeans, a uniform shirt, and set his cowboy hat on his head, leaving his face covered with a day's stubble. He stood out on his deck, drinking a cup of coffee watching the sun come up. The morning mist that hung over the bay hid the low tide. By noon the mist would be gone and the tide would be in.

Ethan contemplated the cycle of life as he watched a seagull dive for food. He rinsed his cup, placed it in the drainer, and locked the door behind him. He drove his black and white 4-wheel drive around the bay to Tillamook.

A small red car parked in the trees off the side of the road caught Ethan's attention. He pulled in behind it and waited a moment to see if the driver was nearby. A strange feeling tugged at his senses. He got on the radio and called in the Washington plate. He was reminded of his dream. He shuddered.

Ethan walked up to the driver's side and looked in. The car was empty and the door was unlocked. He skipped a breath when he noticed the small dream catcher suspended from the rear view mirror.

The dispatcher's voice squawked on his radio. "Sheriff, the car is registered to Mary Dietz, age 26 of Spokane, Washington."

Ethan walked around the car again looking for some sign of the driver or a passenger. None. He glanced around the trees along the road and out into the bay. The roadside was vacant.

Ethan opened the door and poked around inside the car. The back seat was filled with clothes, empty food wrappers, and a woman's makeup bag. The glove box was empty. No registration or insurance documents. He puzzled over the lack of paperwork. He went back to his truck and called dispatch. "Sally, send a tow truck, this car can't stay here. See if you can find some contact information for the registered owner. Thanks,

I'll be in soon." He rubbed his unshaven chin as he sat and waited for the tow truck.

Ethan walked into the small station and hung his hat on the coat rack. Deputy Charlie Enders sat at his desk, surfing the internet.

"Charlie, I want you to do some checking on Mary Dietz, let's see if we can track her down."

"Sure boss." Charlie said.

Ethan sat down and sifted through a stack of paperwork, tapping his pen on the edge of the desk.

Charlie limped across the small office as Ethan poured his second cup of coffee.

"You hurt your leg?" Ethan asked.

"It's nothing, I was painting at the house and fell off a ladder last night." Charlie flipped through pages of his notepad.

"Mary Dietz left her parents' house in Spokane last Thursday, the tenth, heading to Newport to visit a girlfriend, Ellen Cole. I called Miss Cole's number, but Mary hasn't shown up yet. Cole called Mary's cell, but no answer. Said she wasn't too worried because Mary mentioned visiting a couple of other friends on the way."

Ethan put a toothpick in his mouth and rolled it across his tongue. "Did you…"

"I got Mary's cell phone number and called it. I didn't get any answer either. I can't find anyone who has seen her in the last five days." He closed his notepad and rolled his shoulders back.

"Let's notify the state highway boys to watch out for her. See if you can find anyone that saw her leave the car. I know it wasn't there yesterday."

"You got it, boss."

"And Charlie, check around the houses in Bay City, see if she walked up to any of them. Did you get her picture?"

Charlie handed the print to Ethan. "Here you go boss."

The toothpick dropped from Ethan's mouth as he absorbed her photo. It was the young woman from his dream. He folded the picture up. "On second thought, you work with the state troopers, I'll question residents where the car was left."

Charlie shrugged. "You sure boss? Won't take me long to talk to the state troopers. I could help in Bay City."

The Sheriff put on his cowboy hat and looked out the window at rain clouds moving in. "Call me when you're done. We'll see where we're at then." He pulled on his jacket and headed out.

Ethan parked his truck at the center of Bay City and walked the length of the small community. He knocked on every door sharing the picture of the girl that haunted his dreams. They all shook their heads, no one had seen her.

After finishing with the State Police, Charlie questioned the farmers in between, but came back empty handed as well. He met Ethan in a coffee shop in Tillamook in the late afternoon. Charlie looked at the picture of Mary again. "She sure is a pretty thing. Reminds me of my sister."

"You've never talked about a sister, Charlie." Ethan took another drink of coffee.

"Yeah, well, nothing there to talk about."

Ethan sensed Charlie's animosity. "Well I need you to find me some answers to where Mary Dietz is."

Charlie nodded. "I'll go check out the car, see if there's any details that got overlooked."

Ethan swigged the last of his coffee and slipped a dollar bill under the cup. "You do that. I'll see you back in the office later." He gave a polite nod to the waitress and headed out the door. He drove back to the spot where the car had been abandoned and walked the perimeter. The ground beside the road was a bed of old oyster shells. Ethan shuffled through the packed mud and shells looking for anything that could be a clue.

Mayme Divine had one of Ethan's favorite meals ready when he got to her house: pork chops, mashed potatoes and gravy, and homemade biscuits. After their bellies were stuffed, they moved out to the Adirondack chairs on her deck and topped off dinner with red wine as they watched the sun set over the bay.

"You want me to do some digging at the paper?" Mayme asked. Being a columnist for the *Headlight Herald*, gave her an edge on snooping. "I'd be happy to help."

Ethan reached over and put his hand on Mayme's. "Well if you happen to run across something…" He smiled and winked at her.

Mayme laughed. "I'll see if there's anything I can find for you. You want to have lunch tomorrow?"

"I should be able to swing that." He leaned over on one elbow and looked her straight in the eyes. "But darlin', you know what I'd really like?"

She rolled her eyes and looked up to the sky. "Some hot apple pie with a scoop of ice cream?"

"Mayme, I love you. Why won't you marry me?"

"I'm too good for you. Besides, if you were married to me you'd gain four hundred pounds and they'd have to come pick you up with one of those cranes just to move you from room to room." She laughed on her way into the kitchen.

Ethan sat back smiling, inhaling the salty ocean air, embracing the cool evening breeze. Life was so simple and pleasant when he was with Mayme. But even here, in her bed, the dreams would haunt him.

After the sun went down Ethan and Mayme danced barefoot in the living room, then ended the night snuggled in bed. Her two corgis, Elvis and Priscilla curled up on the foot of the bed.

Ethan didn't mind that Mayme's first love was Elvis, as long as he was her second.

As the moon rose in the sky, Priscilla nuzzled her way into the small of Ethan's back. The dream overtook him.

Ethan stood once more on the jetty. A mist from the waves was as cold and sharp as the edge of the rocks. Mary Dietz' car sank into the water; her face trapped inside, frantic, pleading. He reached for her, but his body was paralyzed, and the car was gone. The more he tried to move, the more rigid his body became. He watched a frog with red polka dots hop on the rocks, look up at him, then hop into the water where the car went in.

Ethan turned over quickly when he woke and knocked Priscilla off the bed. She yelped when she hit the floor, then jumped back up on the bed and scooted between him and Mayme. They snuggled again as he fell back asleep.

His internal alarm clock woke Ethan up at half past five. He showered and sat out on the deck with a cup of coffee. Elvis and Priscilla sat at his feet. Mayme came out an hour later.

"I like your deck." Ethan said. "You have a better view of the bay. And it's twice as big as mine."

Mayme sat in the chair next to him with her cup of coffee and smiled. "My house is double the size of yours too."

Ethan looked at his watch and sighed.

"Did you have the dream again?" Mayme asked.

"Yep."

"You have to find her."

He nodded in agreement.

After checking in at the office, Ethan wandered out to the impound lot and searched through Mary Dietz' car. He went through the trunk, glove box, under the seats and in all the small compartments. Nothing new presented itself from the first time he'd looked. There was no clue. Nothing to tell him where she was, or what happened. He glanced up at the rearview mirror.

The dream catcher was gone.

"Boss, what are you doin' out here?" Charlie walked, dragging his hurt leg.

Ethan rubbed his chin and walked around the car. "Do you know where her personal things are?"

"What personal things? We didn't take anything out."

Ethan pointed to the rearview mirror. "There was a small dream catcher hanging there. Where did it go?"

Charlie shrugged. "I didn't notice anything like that, but I can check on it, if you want?"

Ethan looked back inside the car. "Maybe later. What are you doing here?"

"Just lookin' for you, boss."

"Have you had any luck finding anyone who has seen Mary?"

"No sir." Charlie popped a piece of gum in his mouth and chewed on it slow and methodically. "You find anything?"

"No." Ethan replied, wondering.

The two men walked around the corner and into the Sheriff's office. Charlie stopped just inside the door. "Hey boss, I completely forgot, I have a dentist appointment with Doc Roberts in 20 minutes. Just a cleaning, I'll be back in an hour or so." Charlie was gone before Ethan could respond.

Ethan got on the phone to the state police. "This is Sheriff Johnson in Tillamook. My deputy sent over some information yesterday on an abandoned car, and a missing person's report on the driver, a Miss Mary…"

"Sorry Sheriff," the officer on the other end of the line replied, "I haven't received a call from your office in over a week. But I'm happy to help. What's the plates?"

Ethan tapped the pencil vigorously on the side of the desk. He gave the state highway patrol the information on Mary Dietz and her car. He glanced at Charlie's empty desk then poked his head in Sally's office. "Sally, I need you to check on something for me. This is confidential, I want information on Charlie's family. Specifically his sister."

Sally nodded and pulled a folder out of the filing cabinet. "Sheriff, Charlie doesn't have a sister. He doesn't show any family, just his deceased parents."

Ethan stood in the doorway with his hands on his belt. I want you to call around to his last employers, find out if he had a sister, and what happened to her." He turned around and headed back to his desk. "I'm going to check some things out. If Charlie gets back before I do, tell him to stay put."

"Sure thing, Sheriff."

Ethan grabbed his jacket and hat. His movement was halted when he noticed a green rag on Charlie's desk. It was wadded up in such a way, that at first glance it resembled a sitting frog with red splotches on it. "What's this?"

Officer Sam looked over at the rag. "Oh, he had a bloody nose this morning and wiped it with that. You want me to clean it up?"

"No." Ethan said. "I'll put it..." He opened Charlie's desk drawer to slide the rag in, but stopped when he saw a dream catcher poking out from underneath some papers. He pulled it out and found Mary Dietz' car registration underneath it.

"Sam," Ethan said as his jaw tightened.

"Yes Sheriff?"

"I'm going to get a warrant. I want you to check the impound lot video, see if it shows anyone taking stuff out of Dietz' red Mazda, then meet me at Charlie's house in Garibaldi."

It didn't take Ethan more than 30 minutes to get the warrant and head over to Garibaldi to Charlie's small house on 6th street.

Charlie wasn't home. Ethan cautiously slipped around the house looking in the windows. He didn't see anything unusual. He slowly grabbed the back door knob, but it was locked. He pulled out his all-purpose lock tool set and pried the door open.

Charlie's house had a familiar feel to it. He looked around and noticed that all the décor was items he'd seen at Abigail's antique store. But there was nothing to tie him to the missing girl.

Ethan walked back through the kitchen when a floor board creaked under his foot. He stopped, shifted his weight on the boards and listened to the hollow sound underneath. He noticed the lines in the flooring under the small dinette set in the center of the room.

Ethan pushed the table and two chairs aside, revealing a square door in the floor. He unlatched the door and pulled the ring to lift it up. He looked at his watch, it was nearly noon. He opened his cell phone and hit the speed dial number for Mayme.

"It's me. I may be late for lunch today. I'm at Charlie's house right now."

"What are you doing there? Is everything okay?" Mayme asked.

"I think he might be tied to the young woman's disappearance. I'm going to search his cellar right now."

"Does he have a rum runner's cellar? Let me know if you find any old bottles." Mayme chuckled.

"I'll do that. I'll call you as soon as I'm done." He folded the phone and slid it back in his pocket, turned on his flashlight and made his way down the ladder.

The basement was ten by ten feet, dirt and plaster walls. Ethan flashed his light beam along the walls that revealed a heavy plastic protruding from the seams. The room was sealed tight. Wood plank shelves heavy with a smell of old liquor, lined two walls.

Ethan's heart ached as he took in the eight shrines carefully arranged evenly across the dusty spaces. Each collection of objects was dedicated to one woman, with a framed newspaper clipping in the center about a missing woman. A shadow box beside each frame contained articles that were no doubt belonging to the missing woman. A clipping of hair held together with a piece of ribbon, a piece of jewelry, a scrap of torn fabric, and some small trinket.

The last two shrines had an empty frame beside an empty shadow box. But it was the third from the last that bothered Ethan the most, it had a plastic baggie that contained a cutting of light brown hair, a ruby birthstone ring, and Mary Dietz' driver's license. Holy Shit! He thought.

Ethan went back and forth scanning the newspaper articles that spanned over ten years. The last one was reported exactly one year ago, only three months before Charlie joined the

Tillamook Sheriff's Department. He searched the eight shrines for patterns – all eight disappearances occurred in December, all eight women were in their early twenties with light brown hair and brown eyes. The first one gave the most insight, Claire Enders, was found dead in a Las Vegas alley from a drug overdose. In her box was an old photograph from her teenage years, Claire and her brother Charlie, standing arm in arm.

Ethan's attention was diverted when he heard a slam of the back door, and footsteps cross the kitchen. "Sam, is that you?" he called out. But there was no answer, only the sound of the cellar door slamming shut and the latch clicking into place.

Sounds through the floor were muffled, but Ethan could make out the gist of them. He heard the knock on the back door, it must have been Sam. The conversation was short, the door shut, and a car drove off. Next came the sound of heavy furniture being drug across the kitchen floor.

Options ran through Ethan's mind like a grocery checklist. He pulled out his cell phone, but there was no service. He shoved it back in his pocket, sat down on the small chair and turned his flashlight off. Better to save my batteries, he thought.

Ethan coughed; there must have been mold down there, the one thing that would suffocate him. Between the mold and lack of oxygen, he drifted in and out of coherency. His strength was leaving him slowly with every breath. He climbed the small ladder, but could not budge the trap door. Something heavy held it firm, and his strength was fading fast. He slid down the ladder and fell on the floor. He coughed and gasped for air.

Ethan heard a gentle sound in the dark corner, a small choir of angels, surely he was dreaming. A soft light grew out of the blackness, and in the light stood Mary. She held out her hand to him and smiled. "Are you ready?" She asked.

Ethan nodded and coughed. He held out his hand to her and gasped with a ragged breath. He closed his eyes.

A flashlight beam bounced back and forth across the dirt walls. Ethan didn't hear her climb down the ladder and whisper his name. He didn't feel her hand reach out and cradle his face in her palms. But his eyes fluttered as she kissed his lips. There was air, he could breathe, his chest ached.

Mayme smiled at him. "You would be in a world of hurt without me." She kissed Ethan again, then helped him to his feet and up the ladder. He laid his head on her shoulder and coughed.

"Where's Charlie?" Ethan's throat was hoarse.

Mayme sat him on a kitchen chair while she poured him a glass of water. "I don't know. I haven't seen him. I'm sorry it took me so long to get here."

"What time is it?" Ethan sipped the water. "I imagine he's skipped town by now." He looked at the oak desk that sat beside the basement door. "He gave himself a head start."

"It's nearly four o'clock."

Mayme walked Ethan to his car. "You need to get checked out."

Ethan grabbed a Gatorade out of his back seat and took a big swig. "I could really use some coffee, but first things first."

He pulled out his cell phone and scrolled to a number. "Sam, this is Ethan. Have you seen Charlie?"

Sam was still at the station. "Sheriff, where are you? I came to his house but he said you already left."

"Charlie's a killer, Sam. He had me trapped in his cellar when you came by. We need to find him fast."

"Want me to put an APB out on him?"

"Yes. Call me if you find him."

Mayme started to walk over to her car, and looked back at Ethan. "You want me to buy you a cup of coffee? I'll meet you at the Parkside Coffee House."

Ethan smiled. "I'm right behind you, babe."

They sat in the small coffee shop while Ethan ate a late lunch and regained his strength. His cell phone rang. "Hello... which storage units? I'll meet you and Seth there."

Mayme put her cup down. "Was that Sam?"

Ethan leaned forward. "Yep, someone spotted Charlie's rig at the Garibaldi self-storage place."

"Shall I go with you?"

"No, you go home, I'll come by when this is over."

"Are you sure?"

"I gotta' get a warrant for the storage units first. Hopefully he won't have it cleared out before I get back."

Mayme wrinkled her forehead with worry. "It'll be dark soon. You want me to keep an eye out until you can get there? I can park across the road."

Ethan got up and kissed Mayme on the cheek. "Only if you promise to marry me."

Mayme smiled. "We do make a pretty good team."

Ethan grabbed his coat and cowboy hat off the chair beside him.

Mayme gulped another drink of coffee. "Be safe!"

Ethan winked at her as he walked out the door.

It was nearly two hours later when Ethan returned to the small storage units tucked away in the mountain alcove. The place was empty, with a dim light from the one lamp post. Having a unit there himself, he had a key to the main gate. He stopped at the gate and sent Mayme a text. 'Go home and start dinner. See you soon.' He slid the cell phone back in his pocket and turned his flashlight on pointing it at the ground in front of each door. Only one had recent tracks that looked suspicious. Someone with a hurt leg entered unit 14, according to the dragged left footprint in the gravel.

Within a minute, Ethan had the rust proof MasterLock securing unit 14 open. The door growled as it begrudgingly made its way up the track until it reached that magic spot past the bend where it loosened, and sped up to the ceiling where it jarred to a halt. A burst of fowl air rolling out made him gag.

Ethan cautiously walked into the dark, narrow unit. He scanned the space with his flashlight. The west wall was covered from floor to ceiling with plastic bins, neatly stacked and organized by size, shape and color. The east wall held up sports equipment and piled camping gear. Everything here could fit in Charlie's garage, Ethan thought, as he ran the light in a grid from top to bottom, left to right, for the second pass. A few more steps deeper into the space and his light found the back corner.

The flashlight beam stopped on a large piece of black plastic wrapped around something on the bottom rack of a metal shelf.

Ethan knelt down, prayed to be wrong, and pulled the plastic back. His instincts were accurate, as usual.

It was the lifeless body of Mary Dietz.

A vehicle pulled up in the gravel outside. Ethan stood up and saw Charlie's car.

Charlie got out of his car. "Guess you got out of the basement." he snarled.

"Guess you know why I'm here." Ethan rebuked, as he slowly moved his hand to his holster, stepping slowly for the door.

Charlie drew his gun and they fired at each other. Charlie dropped to the ground and Ethan ducked out of the doorway. He listened for a second, no sounds. He cautiously peeked around the corner and Charlie took another shot at him.

"Come on Charlie. There's only one of two ways this is going to end."

"Yeah, boss? Me dead, or you dead."

"I was thinking more of you dead or going to prison."
Charlie laughed. "I'm not going to prison boss, and I don't plan on dying. Not tonight." He shot into the storage unit again.

Head lights from Sam's squad car lit up the parking lot and revealed Charlie hiding behind his car. Charlie shot at the headlights at the same time Ethan fired his gun at Charlie. Sam stopped the car and jumped out, firing a round at Charlie.

All went quiet. Charlie went down.

Ethan came out of the storage unit and walked over to Charlie lying on the gravel, the full moon shining down on his lifeless eyes. "I told you Charlie, one of two ways."

Ethan led Sam into the storage unit, while Seth started marking the crime scene.

Sam holstered his gun and walked into the storage unit with Ethan. "FBI's on their way boss. This guy's left quite a trail."

Beautiful hymns floated on the evening breeze. Ethan turned and watched eight transparent figures smiling at him. They walked toward the bay, disappearing into the night.

Ethan lifted his head to the sky and closed his eyes. He could smell Mayme's hot apple pie in the distance.

Love remains and life prevails.

GHOST HOLLOW

Guilt makes you blind, for while you see one spot of guilt within you, you will not see the light.

It was nearly midnight and the band Cap Gun Suicide had started packing up equipment as the audience filtered out of the Seattle west side concert hall. The spring tour was one show short of ending, and everyone was ready for some down time.

The din of the excited chatter of the exiting crowd was replaced by the barks of band mates and the thud of boots crossing the hollow stage. The loud thunder of music still reverberated in Ted Givens' ears. As the lead guitarist and head of the band, the stress of this tour weighed heavy on his bony shoulders. He needed to clear his head of the sound and the stress. He ducked out the back stage door into the alley and lit up a cigarette as he leaned against the brick wall.

Ted was calmed by the click of the lighter and the glow of the flame. He inhaled gently, while the tip ignited, then deeply, to draw the glow across the end, up the tube and into his cells. He leaned against the brick wall, closed his eyes and took in the warm night air.

Ted opened his eyes to the dark sky, took another soothing drag, and exhaled watching the reflections of street lights shimmer in the puddles from an earlier rain. Relaxed, Ted pushed off the wall to walk down the alley while he finished his smoke.

Nine steps into the shadows he froze and the cigarette dropped from his hand.

Just past the loading dock, in the gap between the wall of the concert hall and the dumpster of the restaurant next door, lay a body, face down, in the still and contorted shape of death.

Thunder rolled in the distance and a drizzle began to fall. Ted looked around in panic, no one else was there. He fell to his knees and reached for the dying ember of the cigarette he had dropped. With the palsy of terror, he slid it between his fingers, took a slow draw then expelled the breath slowly and intentionally through pursed lips. He tightened his jaw, stood up and repeated the process. One last drag and he tossed the cigarette and ground it with his foot as he pushed the air from his chest.

The drops became rain.

Ted took a few steps, gulped, as his eyes locked on the body.

A woman.

The rain mixed with her blood, and ran into the cracks of the broken cement. Ted took yet another step, bent over her and a fresh ticket stub tumbling on the ground below her feet. Cap Gun Suicide admission for one.

Ted kneeled down, slowly reached out and touched her thigh. She was still warm. He could see her face, she was young. His stomach flipped, but he couldn't stop. Her arms, tied behind her, lay at unnatural angles.

Who does this? Ted wondered, as he inched closer to her head. He slid his hands under the once colorful scarf around her neck, and gently tilted her face towards him. The streetlight between the buildings revealed his deepest dread. He gasped as he watched the blood still flowing from the slash circling her neck. Ted's head reeled and his stomach caught in his throat. He turned from the body on all fours to catch his breath. "Holy shit!" he cried as he looked back at the guitar string that still clung to the gash in her throat.

Ted looked left and right in the shadows. He was alone. He stood up, and backed up against the wall, inching his way back to the door, quickly slipping inside the building.

Heather was the bass guitar player, and Ted's wife. Her wavy blond hair was sticking out from under the rhinestone studded hat she wore. She dropped her guitar box on the chair and rushed over to Ted. "What is it? You're as pale as a corpse."

Ted wash shaking as he sat down on the edge of the stage. "Don't say corpse."

Heather sat down beside him. "Ted, you're scaring me. Not another one?" Her expression changed in a second from concern to anger. She stood up trembling with fury.

Ted wiped his wet hair back out of his face. "Call 911, she's dead!"

Trevor latched the case to his keyboard, sat his guitar case on top of it, and turned to look at Ted. "Dead? Another one?" He rubbed his fingers through his bushy mustache.

Ted trembled as he shook his head. "I know. What I don't know is why."

Heather pulled her cell phone out of her bag and called.

Brandon walked over to Ted with his drum sticks still in his hand. He pushed the bandana up that had slid down his forehead. He leaned against the wall. "Same as the girl in Spokane?"

Ted nodded his head. "The same."

Police officers swarmed into the building, flashing pictures and pulling people aside taking statements.

Detective Johnson, a lanky man in a traditional trench coat cornered Ted. "Can you tell me what happened here?" He asked in a way that suggested he already knew.

Ted fumbled with his words through a higher sense of anxiety than before. He looked down at his hands that still had her blood smeared on them. He wiped them as best as he could on his jeans.

Detective Johnson watched Ted's every move. "Son, I have a report here that says you had a young woman murdered the same way, with a guitar string, the night of your concert in Spokane just last week."

Ted fidgeted and shrugged. "Yes sir."

Detective Johnson narrowed his dark eyes on Ted. "You know two for two is not a good sign. You had an alibi in Spokane. But I'm beginning to think this is not just a coincidence."

Ted looked up at the ceiling as if a higher power might save him. "Yes sir."

A police officer pulled the detective aside and talked in a low whisper, then went out the back door. Detective Johnson returned to Ted. "We've already got a sheet going on you and your band members Ted. Your record is clean up to now, but this is not looking good for you."

Ted attempted to swallow but his throat was dry. "Yes sir."

Detective Johnson was getting impatient and his voice began to show the strain, rising in pitch. "Ted, I could book you on murder right now."

Ted looked up into the detective's cold eyes. "I didn't do it. I found her right after we were done with our second set. I didn't see anyone else in the alley, but it wasn't one of us. We were all together." He looked over at Heather.

Detective Johnson wrote some more notes in his pad. "I have your statement and all of your contact information, and I'm telling you right now son, I'm watching you."

It was somber by the time everyone left the building. Ted and his band members loaded the last of their equipment into the old white van and watched the police outside staring at them as they drove away.

Ted drove the van south out of Seattle heading down the coast to Oregon. Heather sat beside him. Trevor and Brandon played cards in the back seat. Ted glanced over at Heather who seemed in a perpetual state of PMS. "I'm glad this tour is almost over, I just want to go home." He said.

She glared at him then lit a cigarette. "No more than I do. Why don't we just go straight home now?"

Ted took a puff off of his cigarette and blew the smoke out the open window. "I told Joe we'd do this gig for him and we're going to."

"This was your idea, not ours." She snapped.

"Hon I told you, Joe and I go way back, I promised him we'd do this. Then we'll go home."

Trevor pulled a card out of the deck between him and Brandon. "Hey Ted, what's this gig for again?"

"Joe said it's for their Garibaldi days. We'll play a set at the marina, have a few beers and head home. It's not a big deal." Ted took another drag off of his cigarette and threw the butt onto the wet pavement out the window. "Trust me, no one wants this trip to end more than me."

Heather huffed as she crossed her arms over her chest. "Really? You've maybe had enough of the band bitching and dead bodies showing up?"

Ted sighed and glanced at the ocean along the highway. He noticed a seagull gliding on the wind, dipping and then flying off out of sight. He wished he could do the same.

Joe lived in a small house just a couple of blocks from the Garibaldi marina. Ted pulled the van into the dirt driveway just before dusk. Joe was sitting on the front step having a beer. He ran up to the van, excited to see his old friend. "'Bout time you showed up!"

"Hey bud, how goes it in sleepy hollow?" Ted got out and started unloading equipment from the van. Heather grabbed her purse and headed into the house without looking up or saying a word.

Joe nodded in her direction. "What's up with the wife?"

Ted let out a heavy sigh. "It's a long story. Let's get the gear inside first, then I'll fill you in."

Brandon put out his cigarette and started pulling out suitcases. "Women, you're nice to them and they hate you, you kill them and they haunt you." He shook his head and carried a load into the house.

Joe looked at Ted with a confused expression. "What the…"

Ted shook his head. "Like I said, it's a long story."

Ted dug into a cooler in the back of the van and pulled a bottle of beer. He twisted off the top and downed it in one large drink. He tossed the empty bottle into a trash sack and pulled another out of the cooler.

Joe helped him carry instruments into the house. "It must be one hell of a story, can't wait to hear it!"

Inside the small house, Ted plopped down on the couch with the beer in his hand and his eyes glazed over. "You have no idea, man. The world has gone insane and it's dragging us down with it."

Joe sat in the chair beside the couch, brushed the hair out of his face. "The others can put everything away. You gotta' tell me what's goin' on, man."

Ted took another drink of beer, let out a sigh and dropped his head back. "I don't even know where to begin. But the cops are watching me and the band."

"What cops?" Joe asked.

"All cops. You know how they are, they're all joined at the hips. Seattle cops, Spokane cops, county mounties, state troopers, cops! Shit, the FBI is probably watching us."

"Okay, so why are all the cops of the world watching you guys? You sang off tune?"

Ted brought his head down and looked Joe straight in the eye. "They think we're murderers."

Joe chuckled as if responding to a joke. "Yeah right. Like I know your music is a killer man, but murder? That's a bit harsh."

Heather came out from the guest bedroom, lighting a cigarette. Her fingers shook. "Harsh isn't the word for it. He's not kidding. Women are getting murdered and the cops have us on a short leash because of it." She walked through the living room, and slammed the front door behind her as she headed out to the front porch.

Joe shook his head in disbelief. "Real murder?"

Ted finished off the beer and set the empty bottle on the floor. "Yes."

"Are the victims people you know?"

"No, that's the weird part. They're just young women who come to the concert, and then they're found dead in the alley afterwards. I don't know them."

"How many?" Joe asked.

Ted rubbed his tired eyes. "Two. One in Spokane and one in Seattle."

"So this is like a serial killing, just women who fit a certain profile?"

"Dude, you've been watching way too much T.V."

Joe barbequed hamburgers on the grill in the back yard, while Ted and Heather set the picnic table. A bucket of ice filled with beer, a stack of paper plates, napkins, buns, chips and condiments.

"Burgers are ready, get 'em while they're hot." Joe called out. Everyone grabbed a plate and started fixing their dinner. They sat at the picnic table eating and drinking. The mood was somber. Ted didn't want to talk about the murders, yet it was the only thing he could think about.

Trevor sat off to the side by himself, scribbling notes on a small spiral pad.

Joe nodded to Trevor. "Hey dude, you writing a new song?"

Trevor ignored him, took a drink of beer, and kept writing.

Joe looked at Ted. "So what about Roger? Wasn't he your main singer? Where's he at these days?

"Roger got arrested for possession. We can't have that in the band. We all got families." "So you just cut him lose?" Joe asked.

"Had to. He didn't give us any choice."

Roger patted Ted on the shoulder. "Dude, you guys gotta' get over this slump. You can't play rock music with this heavy cloud hanging over you."

Heather glared at Joe. "And how do you suppose we get this heavy cloud off? Dude?"

She threw her plate in the trash can and stormed into the house.

Joe shook his head. "Man, this is not right. Look, I will be your body guard here. When you play for our Garibaldi Days shindig, I'll scout the perimeter, all night if I have to, to make sure no one bites the dust at this performance."

Ted finished his burger. "I appreciate it man, I just don't know if you can really stop it."

Joe looked puzzled. "You mean like this is a curse on you guys, or something? Black magic kinda' thing?"

Brandon threw his plate in the trash can as he walked past them into the house. He stopped at the door and looked down at Joe. "It's no curse dude, just some sick bastard, that's all."

Joe laughed. "Well hell, I can take care of that. I deal with those kinda' people all the time!"

Ted smiled at his friend, but inside he was still apprehensive about playing again, and risking another innocent life. His worry showed in the lines on his face.

Joe slapped him on the back and grabbed another beer. "Dude, I'm tellin' you, don't worry. We got you covered!"

Ted nodded. "Hey, it's my job to worry."

The next day drug by for Ted. He cleaned his equipment, inspected everything to make sure it was ready to play at the concert, and went over some songs.

Heather sat at the small kitchen table, smoking cigarettes, glued to her laptop.

Brandon and Trevor were in and out of the house, fidgety and unable to sit and relax. Brandon tapped everything in the house with his drumsticks as he walk by.

Joe looked at his watch. "Hey, we can load up and head to the marina. Come on, I'll help."

They loaded up the van and drove the 3 blocks to the docks where people were gathered for the Garibaldi Days picnic. Ted parked next to a warehouse at the edge of the dock. A younger guy pointed out a spot on the grass for them to set up.

A round balding man stood next to a small building on the grass and greeted everyone. "Okay folks, we've got more fun coming your way with a band out of Boise, Idaho, Cap Gun Suicide." Some of the people cheered and clapped as Ted, Heather, Brandon and Trevor grabbed their instruments and started performing.

Trevor held the microphone in his hand and greeted the small crowd. "This is a song we wrote as a message to kids, it's about being cautious when meeting people over the internet. The song's called *Mable*." Trevor's voice was carried by the ocean breeze across the small marina. People smiled, tapped their feet, and some even stood up to dance.

Ted and the band played for an hour. Joe drank beer and walked around the perimeter of the gathering, keeping his eyes on the band.

The crowd was small. People were busy visiting and eating, and weren't really paying a lot of attention to the music.

When they finished their set, Joe helped the band pack up all the gear and load it back into the van. The sun was just going down and the temperatures were cooling off quickly.

Heather grabbed her hoodie out of the van and pulled it on, zipping it up. "Does it ever get like really warm here?" Her voice was still filled with a high level of irritation.

Joe shrugged. "What are you talking about? This is warm." He laughed. "You in-landers!"

Heather flashed him a dirty look. Joe shivered as if hit with an arctic blast. He laughed it off.

When the gear was packed, they leaned against the van, drinking beer and smoking. Joe looked at his watch. "Hey we should all go to the Ghost Hole and grab a brewski there." He and Ted slapped hands in a high-five motion.

"Come on Ted, you guys know where it's at. Last one there buys the first round!" He laughed as he got in his small pickup and put it into gear.

Ted looked at the rest of the band members. "You guys mind?" He could tell by Heather's expression that she wasn't too excited about it, but Brandon and Trevor got in the van.

"Why not?" Trevor said. "What else do we have to do?"

Heather got in the passenger seat in the front next to Ted. "You mean while we wait the evening out to see if the police are going to come knocking on our door in the morning with yet another murder?"

Trevor slouched down in the back seat.

Brandon took a drag off of his cigarette. "We just want to have a little bit of fun. Try to forget this dark mood for a few hours. Is that so much to ask?"

Heather whipped around and glared at Trevor. "Do you think the families of those dead women mind? Maybe we should ask them if that's too much to ask?"

Ted hadn't pulled out of the parking lot yet. He looked over at Heather. "Hon, lighten up. I know this is bad, we do. No one said it wasn't. But it's not our fault either."

Heather glared at Ted and unhooked her seatbelt, grabbed her shoulder bag and opened her door. "Fine, you go get drunk with your little army bud, I'm going back to the house. Since I'm such a downer to be around right now anyway."

Ted got out of the van and walked over to her. "Hon please. We need to all stay together. This isn't easy on any of us. Besides, I don't want you walking by yourself tonight."

Heather lit a cigarette and took a big drag off of it. "Why, afraid I'll be the next victim?"

Ted pleaded with her. "Heather, hon, that's not funny."

"No, Ted, it's not funny. But I don't feel like hanging out in a bar right now. I just want to be alone. You go bond with your buds, and I'll see you all later." She threw the strap of her purse over her shoulder and headed across the road. "I'll be fine. After all, this is Garibaldi!"

Ted didn't know what to do. He paced for a minute then got in the van. He sat there looking at the side mirror watching his wife walk up the road.

Trevor cleared his throat. "Hey dude, if you want to go with her, we totally understand. Brandon and I can go to the bar and hang out, give you two some alone time."

Ted put the van into gear and drove down to Main Street. "No, I need a beer."

Inside the small bar the guys drank, played darts, and told stories. The bar was small and crowded. A mid-fifties couple sang a variety of tunes from Proud Mary to Family Affair on the small Karaoke stage.

Ted stood at the bar waiting for a refill on his beer. He glanced up at the mirror behind the bar and saw a dark hooded figure standing behind him. He spun around to look at who it was, but when he turned, the hooded figure was gone. He looked all over the small room, but no one fit the image he had seen in the mirror. He walked back to the table with the other guys.

"Listen, I think I've had enough. You guys take the van, I'm walking back to the house. I'm worried about Heather."

"Dude," slurred Joe, "you worry too much. Man, sit down and have another beer. She's fine. Besides, if the devil was dumb enough to mess with your wife, I'd have to say my money's on her!"

Joe laughed and held up his glass in a toast. "No doubt man, Heather could kick any ass. That woman scares me just looking at her."

Ted grabbed his jacket off the back of the chair. "Yeah well, I'm going home to check on her."

Ted walked out of the bar and crossed the road. The small town was quiet, no traffic or noise. His footsteps sounded ten times louder than normal, echoing through the whole neighborhood. He looked up the block and saw the hooded figure standing under the streetlight. He panicked more with every step as he broke into a run to the house.

As Ted rounded the corner to Joe's house, he heard a woman scream. The sound made his blood run cold. It was Heather!

He sprinted to the house, racing time to reach her before death did. He rushed in the front door panting. He darted through the small house. "Heather! Where are you?" he yelled between gasps for air.

Ted heard another scream! He stopped to catch his breath. Where did the scream come from? His heart pounded out the terror in his mind. He ran out the back door into the alley. He saw a movement behind a garbage can.

The moonlight peaked through the clouds revealing the body sprawled out in the gravel.

Ted dropped to his knees and held Heather's head, holding a hand over the deep gash in her neck. She was still alive. He rested her head in his lap, pulled his cell phone out of his pocket, and hit the speed dial for Joe.

"Heather's in the alley behind the house. Her throat's been cut. Get an ambulance here right away!" He dropped the phone and rocked her in his arms.

"It's okay hon, help is on the way. You're going to be okay. I've got you now." He softly sang *Heather's Song* to her, a song he'd written for their wedding. The words crackled through his fear and heartbreak.

Sirens blared through the quiet night as they entered the alley and found their way to Ted and Heather. The EMTs quickly taped up the gash in her neck, sliding her on a gurney.

Ted stood up, covered in blood, his face wet with tears. "Is she going to be okay? Please tell me she's going to be okay?"

Sheriff Johnson pulled up in his pickup from the other end of the alley. He motioned for the ambulance to leave and looked at Ted. "What happened son?"

Ted let out a shaky breath. "I don't know. I was at the bar with my friends, and I just got this horrible feeling that something was wrong. So I headed to the house and I heard a scream." He wiped his hair back, smearing blood across his face. "She wasn't in the house, so I ran out here and I saw something move. Then I saw her lying on the ground covered in blood."

"You're in the band that played at the park earlier this evening, aren't you?"

"Yes, my wife's the bass player."

"Where's the weapon? What was she cut with?" Sheriff Johnson flashed his flashlight back and forth across the gravel.

"Her throat was cut with a guitar string."

"Where is it?"

"I don't know."

"Then how do you know that was the weapon?" Just then, the sheriff saw the glimmer of something bloody in the rocks. He pulled out a rubber glove to pick it up.

"Because that's what the others were killed with. Their throats were slit with guitar strings. She's going to be okay, isn't she? Can I go see her now?"

Sheriff Johnson stood up and pointed his flashlight directly into Ted's face. "What do you mean, the others? Did you do this?" He started to reach slowly for his gun.

"No. I don't know who's doing it. I just know they're using guitar strings."

"Come on," Sheriff Johnson said, "get in my truck; I'll drive you over to the hospital."

Ted was in a daze as they drove around the bay from Garibaldi to Tillamook. He kept mumbling to himself, "she's going to be okay."

At the hospital, Ted washed his hands and face. His sweatshirt was still smeared with Heather's blood. He sat in the waiting room while they worked on Heather.

Sheriff Johnson sat down next to Ted. "Listen son, I did some checking, and you've had a rash of these murders in your wake. What can you tell me about it?"

Joe, Trevor and Brandon all rushed into the waiting room.

Joe was out of breath. "Dude, is she okay? Like Heather's not going to die, is she?"

Trevor sat down on the other sided of Ted. "Man, I know this sounds crazy, but I'd swear right after you left I saw Roger standing in the corner of the bar. He was dressed in a black hooded sweatshirt, but when I got up to go talk to him, it was like he just vanished. Dude, you think this is Roger?"

"Who's Roger?" Sheriff Johnson asked.

Ted looked up at the sheriff. "Roger used to be the lead singer of our band, before Trevor. But he got caught doing drugs and we cut him loose. We don't do that shit. And we all have families, we didn't want that karma. You know?"

"What's his last name?"

Trevor pulled out his cell phone. "Roger Billings. Here's his phone number. Man, do you really think Roger would do this though? I mean like killing innocent women? And Heather?"

Ted shook his head. "I don't know anymore. I don't know what Roger would do, or if it was him."

Sheriff Johnson got up and called the station with the information on Roger.

A doctor came out in blood covered scrubs. "Is Heather's husband out here?"

Ted jumped up out of his chair. "That's me, I'm Ted, I'm her husband. She's okay, right?"

The doctor smiled at Ted. "Your wife is stable. She's going to have a nasty scar on her neck, and she did lose a lot of blood. She's going to have to stay in here until we get everything under control. She's getting a transfusion right now, and she's got a mess around her vocal chords."

Ted grabbed the doctor's hands to shake them. "Thank you, thank you so much. Can I go see her now?"

"Not yet. You'll need to talk to the admissions clerk and get all that squared away, and by then they should have her in a room." He patted Ted on the shoulder and headed back down the hall.

Sheriff Johnson came back in about a half hour later with a confused look on his face. "Boys, I've got some disturbing news."

Ted didn't have a good feeling about this. "Yeah? What news?"

"Your friend, Roger, committed suicide three weeks ago. He managed to hang himself with a guitar string." He peered at Ted and the others as he rolled a toothpick back and forth across his tongue. "You got any other ideas?"

Ted gulped.

Joe spoke up. "Dude, I told you this was black magic! Like how else could he kill those other ladies and attack Heather?"

The sheriff tilted his head. "Joe, it wasn't a ghost that attacked her. I need to get each of your statements for this evening." He sat down with a notepad in his hands. "Tell me what happened tonight."

"Sheriff, we were all at the Ghost Hole, except Heather. She went back to my place."

"By herself?"

Ted spoke up. "Yes. She didn't want to go to the bar. And then about eleven or ten after eleven, I left and walked up to Joe's. 'Cause we're staying with them. And I heard her scream and found her in the alley. You already know that."

Sheriff Johnson peered into Ted's bloodshot eyes. "So you were not with the others when she was attacked?"

Joe just about slipped out of his chair from all the alcohol he'd drank. "Dude, are you saying Ted tried to kill his own wife? Whoa! That's just sick and wrong!"

"I did not attack my wife! Someone else did."

Sheriff Johnson looked down at his notes. "But no one else was there except for you."

Ted fell back in his chair exasperated. "I'm telling you, it wasn't me."

Sheriff Johnson stood up. "Come on son, I'm sorry, but evidence talks pretty loud. And it's telling me I need to lock you up right now."

Joe stood up in protest. "Sheriff, there's no way Ted did this. It's like Ghost Hollow."

Sheriff Johnson handcuffed Ted. "Joe, Ghost Hollow is an old legend, nothing more." He guided Ted out the door.

Trevor stood up and looked at Joe. "What's Ghost Hollow?"

"Ghost Hollow's a place between here and Garibaldi. They found a man dead there once. You know, one of those unsolved mysteries."

Ted listened to his friends as he walked out of the hospital with the sheriff. He looked up at Sheriff Johnson. "I didn't do it Sheriff. I love my wife. I was only trying to protect her."

Sheriff Johnson only nodded as they continued to his truck.

Early the following morning, after breakfast had been served, Zoey walked up to Ted's jail cell with a guard.

"Hi Ted, my name is Zoey Jacobs and I work for the *Headlight Herald*. I understand your wife was attacked by a serial killer yesterday in Garibaldi. Can you tell me anything about that?"

Ted looked at her like she was crazy. "What in the hell are you talking about? What serial killer? Where's my lawyer?"

"It's okay. I want to get as many of the facts for the paper as possible. But you did have two murders by the same attacker after recent concerts, correct?" Zoey wrote some notes down on a small pad.

"I want out of here. I need to see my wife. Guard!" Ted yelled.

"And all the murders, as I understand it, were done with your guitar string?" Zoey said.

"Look lady, I don't know who you are, and I don't feel like discussing this with you."

"I told you, I'm Zoey Jacobs with the *Headlight Herald*. This is quite an intriguing story, don't you want the truth?"

Ted drew up his hand to shield his face. "I already know the truth. Now leave me alone."

"I can come back later." Zoey shrugged, put her notepad away, and walked down the hall. But her steps were halted by a haunting sensation that crawled across her skin, as she heard a soft voice behind her hum a familiar song.

Row, row, row your boat, gently down the stream. Merrily, merrily, merrily, merrily, life is but a dream.

Life is but a dream.

***

185

I hope you enjoyed the stories and lives of the fictional people of Garibaldi. I welcome your words, thoughts and reviews.

www.SherryBriscoe.com

Made in the USA
San Bernardino, CA
29 June 2014